WHEN LULU WAS HOT

CAJUN SERIES PREQUEL

SANDRA HILL

SH
BOOKS

"Hill will tickle readers' funny bones yet again as she writes in her trademark sexy style. A real crowd-pleaser, guar-an-teed."

—*Booklist* (starred review, on *The Cajun Cowboy*)

"Hill's thigh-slapping humor and thoughtful look at the endangered Louisiana bayou ecosystem turn this into an engaging read."

—*Publishers Weekly*, on *The Red-Hot Cajun*

"4 Stars! A hoot and a half! Snappy dialogue and outrageous characters keep the tempo lively and the humor infectious in this crazy adventure story. Hill is a master at taking outlandish situations and making them laugh-out-loud funny."

—*Romantic Times BOOKreviews Magazine* on *Pink Jinx*, a *USA Today* bestseller

"The riotous cast of characters...will keep you laughing from cover to cover...passionate encounters keep the sexual tension at a steady boil. The outlandish adventures of this wacky, wonderful family will make you wish you lived on the bayou!"

—*FreshFiction.com*, on *Wild Jinx*, a *New York Times* bestseller and one of *Booklist*'s Top Ten Romances of 2008

"Hill offers fun stories with lots of local color and sexual attraction."

—The Houma, Louisiana "Advertiser" on *So Into You* (retitled *Bayou Angel*)

"With Sandra Hill you'll be laughing out loud at one moment and crying the next. But most of all you'll be smiling as her books just wrap themselves around your heart. Yes, these stories are like taking happy pills and *Snow on the Bayou* is one of the sweetest medicines around."

—FabFantasyFiction.com on *Snow on the Bayou*

"Sandra Hill will have readers laughing—and crying!— through the bayous of her latest Cajun novel. Thanks to her witty metaphor-galore dialogue, eclectic characters and massive pet menagerie, she'll have her audience craving sweet tea and a trip to the south in no time."

—*Romantic Times BOOKreviews Magazine* on *The Cajun Doctor*

Print ISBN: 978-1-941528-55-6

Publisher: Parker Hayden Media
Imprint: Sandra Hill Books

Art credits:
Cover Design: LB Hayden
Cover model: Zoomteam (Depositphotos)

This book is dedicated to all you loyal fans of my Cajun series who have begged me for years to give Tante Lulu her very own book. I resisted because there was tragedy in her life, what she called her Big Grief, and I write humor.

But then, I recalled what a wise editor once told me. In the best of all novels, the writer makes the reader cry, as well as laugh. So, that's what I wish for you in this book. Tears and laughter. But mostly laughter.

God bless Tante Lulu!

Don't we all wish we had a relative like her in our own families?

Present Day
Sentimental Journey...

*L*ouise Rivard, best known up and down the bayou as Tante Lulu, was celebrating her ninetieth birthday. For the second year in a row.

Or was it the third?

Maybe the fourth.

Whatever! she thought. *Age is just a number, like I always say. Some fools are old fogies at fifty, like rusted-out jalopies, bless their hearts, creepin' along the highway of life. Me, on the other hand, I still have a bucket-load of va-voom under my hood, and miles to go before I bite the dust.*

Bucket-load, bucket list, get it?

Ha, ha, ha! There's a hole in my bucket, there's a hole in my bucket...

Talking to herself was nothing new for Louise. Answering herself was another matter, especially when she answered in song. And, no, it had nothing to do with her age or that alls-hammer some seniors got. It was just that sometimes she was more fun than the people around her; so, she had to amuse herself.

Anyways, like she told her niece Charmaine last week, "Ninety is the new seventy."

"If that's true, then forty is the new twenty. Hal-le-lu-jah! Heck, I'll settle fer thirty." Charmaine, ever conscious of her age and appearance, had done a little boogie dance around Louise's kitchen to celebrate. "Maybe I'll have T-shirts made up fer mah beauty spas with that message. 'Forty Is the New Thirty' on the front, and on the back, 'And We Can Help. Cut & Die Hair Salon, Houma, Louisiana.'"

Charmaine owned a string of hair salons and beauty spas in Southern Louisiana. A self-proclaimed bimbo with a brain, she was always looking out for the main chance.

Which isn't a bad thing, necessarily, in my opinion.

Actually, Louise's birthday had already passed, and been celebrated in grand style with a pool party at her nephew Luc's house. Even so, today her LeDeux great-nephews and -nieces, along with a few great-greats, were treating her to a belated gift, some kind of secret destination road trip. There were so many of the family tagging along that they were a highway caravan. Pick-up trucks, expensive sedans like Luc's BMW, even Louise's vintage, lavender Chevy Impala convertible, named Lillian, being driven by her great-great-niece Mary Lou, who was constantly pleading for first dibs on the vehicle in Louise's will.

To which, Louise always answered, "I ain't dead yet, girl. Mebbe I'll get buried in it, 'stead of some boring wood casket. Wouldn't that shock St. Peter if I came roarin' through the Pearly Gates? Not to worry. St. Jude would be out front, wavin' me in."

St. Jude was Louise's favorite go-to saint, the patron of hopeless cases. And, whoo-boy, had she run into a passel of hopeless folks in her time! Herself included, especially after...well, a long time ago.

Louise was riding shotgun in the first vehicle, an SUV driven by her youngest LeDeux nephew, Tee-John, "tee-" being a Cajun prefix for small or little. Not so young anymore, Tee-John, a cop from up Lafayette way, was what modern people called thirty-something. And he was far from little anymore, either.

Tee-John's wife Celine sat in the back seat with their son, Etienne, who was thirteen going on twenty, a rascal just like his daddy had been...and probably still was. Lately, Etienne insisted that his friends call him by the English version of his name, Steven. If Louise heard, "Call me Steve," one more time when she talked to him, she was going to pitch a hissy fit.

"Ay-T-en is a perfectly good Cajun name, and you're Cajun ta the bone, boy," she often told him.

The rascal usually winked at her and said with an

3

exaggerated drawl, "Ah know, auntie. Cantcha tell, ah got mah Cajun on all the time, guar-an-teed!"

As a contrast to their older brother, six- and five-year-old Annie and Rob were in the way-back seat, deaf to their surroundings with headsets connected to games on their cell phones. Etienne was expertly thumbing his way on his own phone, too, even as he talked. A multitasker!

What was the world coming to when children needed their own phones? Knowing Etienne, he was probably looking at nekkid pictures, or sending ones of himself. Lordy, Lordy, the boy was a trial. Girls up and down the bayou best beware when this boy got old enough to really get his Cajun on.

"Do you wanna know what yer surprise birthday gift is, auntie?" Tee-John asked her, once they were on the road.

"No, I wanna sit on my hiney playin' twenty questions," she griped. A trip to Baton Rouge was not her idea of fun, even if they went to some fancy pancy restaurant, or visited some historic site, or something else her family had in mind, like they usually did. She'd rather be working in her garden (she had two bushels of figs ready to be picked), or practicing her belly dancing (there was a competition coming up soon that she was thinking about entering), or playing bingo at Our Lady of the Bayou Church hall (where the jackpot this week was a Crock-Pot big enough to hold a small pig).

Ooh, ooh, ooh, an idea suddenly came to her. "Is Richard Simmons in town? Am I finally gonna meet my crush?" Since the exercise guru had disappeared from the public eye in recent years, she'd been worried about him.

Tee-John rolled his eyes, and she heard snickering from Celine. "Who's Richard Simmons?" Call-me-Steve asked.

She shook her head with disgust. No one understood her longtime fascination with the exercise celebrity. She knew Richard hadn't been handsome in the traditional sense, even when he was younger, but he had a positive attitude about life that she loved. And he had va-voom if anyone did! His jumping jacks still gave her tingles.

"No, you're not gonna meet the famous Richard," Tee-John said. "Your gift is a visit to a reenactment type event in Baton Rouge called, 'The War Years: A Celebration'."

"Big whoop! Another Civil War re-enactment! When are Southerners gonna realize they lost that war? And why would ya imagine I'd be interested? You'd think I lived back then, the way some folks keep bringin' it up. 'Didja ever meet Jefferson Davis, Tante Lulu? Ha, ha, ha!' I ain't that old!"

Etienne muttered something that sounded like "Wanna bet?"

She turned and threatened to swat "Call me Steve" with her St. Jude fan, then told Tee-John, "Besides, ya keep tellin' me it's politically incorrect ta refer ta Northerners as Damn Yankees anymore. So, why we gonna celebrate that war again? We, fer certain, cain't be wavin' no Confederate flags, 'less we wanna be called big-hots."

Tee-John was laughing so hard he'd probably be peeing his pants. "You mean bigot, auntie. Not big-hot."

"I know what a bigot is, fool."

"Why do you bother correcting her?" Celine asked her husband, as if Louise wasn't even there.

Actually, Celine, and all the other LeDeux women for that matter—Sylvie, Rachel, Val, and Charmaine—were kind of mad at Louise, claiming that she had put a curse on them to make them all pregnant at this late stage in their lives. All Louise did was make a chance remark to St. Jude, in their hearing, that it would be nice to have more babies around.

Last summer, they were sure they were all breeding, then the next month they weren't, then they were, now no one was sure. Samantha was the only one not complaining, but she and Daniel were just getting started

How they could blame her for their wonky cycles was beyond Louise. It was all up to God...and St. Jude, of course. And, besides, everyone knew children were a blessing, not a curse.

In any case, Louise ignored Celine's snarkiness and continued, "As fer grown men playin' war games with antique guns? Pfft! And I ain't gonna sit around watchin' grown men whistle 'Dixie,' either, like we did at the Shrimp Festival last year."

Celine kept trying to interrupt her, and finally got a few words in. "Not that war, Tante Lulu."

"And, FYI, I don't think there were many Johnny Rebs who took the time to whistle during the Civil War," Tee-John added, before she shut them both up.

"Do ya think I'm a total idjit? I'd like ta f. y. i. ya with my f. a. n."

Tee-John grinned.

Celine explained with a long sigh, as if Louise was the idjit in this car, and not them, "This is about the World War II era. There will be all kinds of venues related to the 1940s. Music, clothing, movies, dances, everything involving the home front."

Tee-John backed his wife up by telling Louise, "You're always tellin' us stories about that time, when you were single. We thought you'd enjoy it."

"Hmpfh! How'd ya hear about this?"

"A brochure came into the newspaper office, and I volunteered to cover the event." Celine was a feature reporter for the *Times Picayune* in New Orleans. "It's the first ever for Loo-zee-anna, but these kind of World War II celebrations are very popular all over the world, especially in Britain."

"Isn't there a World War II museum in Nawleans?" Louise asked.

"Yes, but this is different," Celine said.

"People want to go back to a time when life was simpler and country pride was at a high," Tee-John elaborated.

"Ya mean like Donald Trump wantin' ta make America proud again?"

"Not even close," Tee-John said with a laugh. "The 1940s were a time of austerity, as you well know. And people showed their pride and did their part by planting

Victory Gardens, home canning, using ration books buying war bonds."

"I still have a garden, and I still can fruit and vegetables," Louise said. "Big deal!"

Tee-John was the one sighing now. "We figured you were a young woman back then, and this event would bring back memories."

He had no idea! The years from 1942 to 1944 were the happiest and most tragic of her life, leading to what she called her Big Grief. She would never forget. And she didn't need any old war fair to jog her memories.

"It'll be fun," Celine said.

I'd rather stick needles in my eyes or watch a cypress tree grow.

"I hope they have tanks. I always wanted to climb into one of those tanks and shoot off a dozen rounds. Bam, bam, bam!" Steve/Etienne said.

"Don't ya dare climb up on any machinery," Tee-John warned. "You're already grounded fer that tattoo incident."

Tante Lulu chuckled. It was payback time for Tee-John, the wildest boy in the bayou. "Talk about bein' grounded, I remember the time ya went ta that clothing-optional party, Tee-John, when ya were little more'n Etienne's age."

"Auntie!" Etienne protested. "Call me Steve."

Tee-John groaned. "Did you hafta mention that party?"

Celine laughed.

"Whoa!" Etienne hooted. "Tell me more."

"It wasn't clothing-optional, it was underwear-optional," Tee-John corrected.

"Oh, that's better. Not!" Celine remarked.

"I'm not wearing any underwear," Etienne informed them all.

Every person in the car looked at the boy, even his father through the rearview mirror, and the two "robots" in the way-back who pretended to be brain dead from cell phoneitis, but, apparently, heard everything. But no one said anything. What *could* you say to that?"

Doesn't it hurt?" Rob asked finally. "One time I went ta school without my underwear 'cause my Superman tightie whities were dirty, and the zipper on my jeans chafed my tooter somethin' awful."

"Ya shoulda put some of my snake oil ointment on it," Louise advised.

"Ouch!" Etienne said. "You're supposed ta arrange yer goodies ta the side."

"Goodies? Eew!" Annie observed.

"Oh," was Rob's reaction. "How do ya do that arrangin' thing?"

"That's enough on the subject," Tee-John ordered.

"Talk about!" Louise remarked.

And Celine smacked her son on the shoulder.

"What did I do?" Etienne asked, but he was grinning like a pig in honey-coated slop.

When they parked in the State Fairgrounds lot, a huge banner did, indeed, announce, "The War Years: A Celebration," and Louise thought of something. "Y'know, Tee-John, lots of pacifists would be offended at a celebration of that war. It wasn't all swing music and pretty hair-dos. There was some grim stuff goin' on back then. Yessirree. Like the Holocaust and Hiroshima, not ta mention all the soldiers that got killed." Including one near and dear to her own heart, she couldn't help but think. "'Course, we dint know 'bout the concentration camps and big bombs and all that till the end."

"I can answer that," Celine said.

Surprise, surprise!

"The event promoters put out a disclaimer ahead of time, stating that the war itself wasn't being celebrated, but the home front and the culture of the times," Celine went on.

Doesn't she always? Go on, and on, and on.

"In fact, they're making every effort to show respect for those who died and the vets who survived with special activities, like an honor guard of remaining World War II veterans, a D-Day commemoration, and so on."

"You're right, though, auntie. We shouldn't look at the war with rose-colored glasses," Tee-John said, as he helped her out from the high seat. She was barely five feet tall in her bare feet. Auto makers were prejudiced against short people, if you asked her. She used to be five-foot-three...well, five-foot-two-and-a-half, but somehow the inches were disappearing, along with her boobs and butt.

Immediately, Annie took her one hand and Rob, the other. They really were sweet children. Maybe these two wouldn't turn out as wild as Tee-John and Etienne. And Celine wasn't so bad, either, Louise had to admit, espe-

WHEN LULU WAS HOT

cially if she could raise up three good children like these three. Or put up with Tee-John's antics, truth to tell.

Hundreds, maybe thousands, of people were strolling about the grounds. They followed the crowds.

A map of the fairgrounds showed where particular booths were situated, like vintage clothing, hair styling, music, movies, kitchen gadgets, food, Victory Gardens, toys, penny arcades, ration books, tea rooms, and picture booths. There would be a parade of classic cars later in the day.

"Lillian is a classic. She could be in the parade," Louise said.

"She isn't old enough, auntie," Tee-John said.

Louise didn't hear that very often, about herself anyway.

Despite what Celine had said, there was a lot of military stuff going on, Louise noticed, studying the roster some more, like a war bonds poster booth, displays of service uniforms, guns and ammo, aircraft, WACs, USOs, and historical booths that included a number of authors and the books they'd written about the war. Like the vintage cars, there would be a convoy of military vehicles.

At the far end of the grounds there was a stage where various swing bands would be playing, with a Bob Hope impersonator running the show. In addition, making an appearance would be Radio Josette, the Voice of the South, who had been popular with local servicemen back in the 40s.

"I thought Josette Sonnier died twenty years ago.

Josie was usin' a walker at a fifty-year D-Day commemoration back in 1994. She mus' be ancient by now."

Etienne snickered behind her, as if her calling someone ancient was funny. She ignored him, for now, and explained, "Josie was a beauty, but mostly the fellows loved her 'cause she had this soft, sexy voice with a Southern accent. Made the homesick soldiers feel like there was allus someone waitin' fer them ta come back after the war."

To demonstrate, she lowered her voice and imitated Josie's usual greeting to her radio fans. "Hel-lo, boys! This is Radio Jo-sette comin' ta y'all from Loo-zee-anna. I've got somethin' fer ya, fellas, y'hear?"

Etienne wasn't snickering now. In fact, he was staring googly-eyed at her, while Tee-John was laughing like a drunk hyena.

But then, their attention was diverted to her niece Charmaine who'd joined them after emerging from a pick-up truck with the logo "Triple L Ranch," along with her husband Raoul "Rusty" Lanier and their daughter Mary Lou. Rusty and Mary Lou wore typical cowboy/cowgirl attire...denim pants and shirts, well-worn boots and hats. But Charmaine...Lordy, Lordy!...was dressed like a 1940s pin-up. And, believe it or not, Louise knew a lot about 1940s pin-ups. It didn't matter that Charmaine had hit the forty mark by now. As a former Miss Louisiana, she had an image to maintain. Face it, she was still hot as Cajun Lightning, or Tabasco sauce, the South's contribution to the world of spice.

Charmaine must have inherited Louise's genetic

taste for outrageousness because she was wearing red, high-heeled, peep-toe pumps with seamed stockings. A white blouse with shoulder pads, unbuttoned to expose her famous cleavage, was tucked into a slim—very slim— black skirt that hugged her butt cheeks. A wide, red patent-leather belt cinched in her waist. Her long, black, wavy hair was tucked behind one ear and hung over the other eye, Veronica Lake style, topped by a pert little red pillbox hat with a half veil. Her make-up was expertly applied as usual to look natural, except for her favorite Crimson Fire lipstick. There wasn't a woman alive who could do justice to shiny red lipstick like Charmaine.

Rusty, the handsomest Cajun man to walk on two feet (everyone said so), looked as if he'd like to eat her up, like he always did. Crazy in love with his wife the boy had been for twenty years now.

If Charmaine was preggers, she sure was hiding it.

And there came Remy and his family...some of them anyways. There were a whole passel of them, including Andy LeDeux, the baseball player, who immediately had fans surrounding him, asking for autographs. Remy would have been just as good looking as Rusty, except, as a pilot during Desert Storm, he'd suffered massive burns, but only on one side of his body, forehead to toes. A shame, that! But he'd survived, that was the most important thing. Besides, to her, and to his adoring wife Rachel, he was still good-looking. And a hero.

Despite all their children, mostly adopted, Louise knew that Remy and Rachel would welcome more. But then, Rachel wasn't looking any fatter, either.

Her oldest nephew, Luc, and his wife Sylvie came too, with their three daughters. Next to Tee-John, Luc was her favorite. As a young boy, he'd practically raised his brothers in a rusted-out trailer with no running water. Louise had rescued the boys from their abusive father, that devil Valcour LeDeux, and saved herself in the process.

Luc had a vasectomy a few years back. What a joke it would be on him if God...or St. Jude...stuck out a big toe and tripped him up! If God could raise the dead, he could surely undo a few of man's snips.

Finally came René and his two kids, Jude and Louise. Louise had a particular affection for these two little ones...Louise because the little girl was her name-sake, and Jude because he was named after her favorite saint.

René's wife Val, a lawyer, was in court this morning, representing a woman accused of assaulting her low-life drunk of a husband. "Some men just need killing" was considered a legal defense in some parts of Louisiana. Or, "Some lowlifes jist need a good whompin'," Louise often said.

Val was the one the most upset with Louise over this whole I'm pregnant/I'm not pregnant issue. Val was the type of woman who thought she could control her life, without any help from Above, or even from down the bayou, meaning Louise.

René, an environmentalist and teacher, was also a musi-cian—a member of the Swamp Rats, a popular bayou band.

He headed immediately for the booth showcasing music of the World War II era. Old vinyl records and albums were being sold to a long line of customers, which was surprising since everyone today seemed to be getting their music from wires hanging from their ears. She wondered how anyone could play these records since stereos were obsolete. Heck, even eight-track tape players, cassettes, and CDs were outdated. *Too bad! It's a cryin' shame that we live in a throw-away society now. Toss it out if it shows any age. In fact, they'd throw old people out, too, if they could.*

But wait, the vendor was also selling antique record players, as well as modern reproductions, some of them inside actual furniture, like those old stereo cabinets, one of which she still had in her living room. Maybe the young'uns in her family would stop making fun of her after seeing this.

Another booth displayed collectible Bakelite radios. She had one of those, too—a Philco tabletop model that still played just fine.

The music was a wonderful backdrop for this event, but it caused the fine hairs to stand out all over her body, and she felt kind of lightheaded. She held onto Charmaine's arm as they walked along. The old sappy favorites, like "Stardust," "I'll Be Seeing You," and "Sentimental Journey," and even the more upbeat ones, like "Chattanooga Choo-Choo," and "Boogie Woogie Bugle Boy," they all triggered memories almost too painful to bear. Louise realized that she'd unconsciously avoided those songs over the decades in favor of the traditional

French Cajun music, or zydeco, of the bayou. Now she knew why.

Etienne...rather, Steve...went off with his Daddy to look at all the military stuff, including, yes, a few tanks. Tee-John probably accompanied him so he wouldn't really climb into one of the things.

Next up was a booth about Victory Gardens and home canning. Hah! Cajuns, ever frugal, knew all about the benefits of raising their own food. There was even a booth about bayou animals, how to catch and cook them, including squirrels, raccoons, snakes...and gators, of course.

"There's a trend toward austerity t'day," Charmaine told her, using the same word Tee-John had, back in the car. "People wanna go back ta simpler lifestyles. Avoid processed foods and red meat. Live off the land, completely."

"Whass wrong with a supermarket once in awhile?" Louise asked. "And ain't nothin' like a rare roast beef with sides of okra and dirty rice."

"I cain't argue with that, livin' on a ranch and all. Right, Rusty?" Charmaine asked.

But Rusty and Mary Lou had already moved on to the next booth where an old-fashioned wringer-type washing machine was being demonstrated.

"I remember those. What a pain in the hiney they were! Took half a day jist ta do a little laundry. 'Course, Monday was allus wash day. And we allus had red beans an' rice simmerin' on the stove on Mondays 'cause it took no trouble."

Rob and Annie were fascinated by a Pez booth with samples of hundreds of the candy dispensers. An old Woolworth sign advertised them for ten cents each. She could only imagine what those early ones were worth today.

Cigarette girls walked around the grounds with trays held by a neck strap. Camels, Lucky Strikes, Pall Malls, Raleighs. They were probably empty packs, considering their reputation as "coffin nails," but there was no question they had been popular back in the day. She'd smoked a few herself, when she'd thought they made her look older and more sophisticated.

Separate booths dealt with ration books, Spam, Griswold cast-iron pans, and kitchen gadgets. Louise had to explain to Mary Lou the purpose of ice picks, hand-cranked meat grinders, and treadle sewing machines.

All the women and girls were fascinated by the vintage clothing on display. Both Sylvie and Rachel sat down to have their hair styled in "Victory Rolls" that ran from one ear, along the nape, to the other ear, with center parts, or cute bangs across their foreheads. Still others had their hair done into an "up-do."

Meanwhile, among the crowds, Celine pointed out that there were educators here who wanted to impart information about the era (the event organizers, historical societies, professors, and authors), men who liked boy toys (the military paraphernalia, in particular), and the promenaders (military re-enactors and people who just loved the attire of that time period, like Charmaine).

SANDRA HILL

Occasional World War II vets also hobbled about. Actually, veterans of other wars, as well.

Louise was particularly touched when she noticed some fellows in the old white "crackerjack" uniforms of the sailors, complete with the "Dixie Cup" or "gob" hats that could be molded to a rakish angle. The memories they triggered caused her heart to constrict so tight she could barely breathe.

"Are you all right?" Tee-John asked, coming to stand beside her. Apparently he and Etienne were done ogling the war planes and tanks.

"I'm fine," she replied, but looped her arm in his as they moved along.

"Holy shit!" Etienne said suddenly.

"Watch yer language." His father smacked him on his shoulder.

"Sorry," Etienne apologized, though he didn't look sorry at all. Instead, he pointed to a tent that had a display of 40s pin-up posters and magazine covers, including some by the famous painter Alberto Vargas.

"Lookee there, Tante Lulu was a centerfold."

"She was not!" Tee-John declared, giving his son another smack.

"Yes, I was," Tante Lulu said.

"Told ya!" Etienne hooted. "That chick up there looks jist lak Tante Lulu in that graduation picture on her dresser...the one in a silver frame. Y'know the one I mean, Daddy. She's wearin' a red dress and high heels and holdin' a diploma."

"I'll be damned!" Tee-John muttered.

Everyone in her family who'd gathered to see what the problem was turned as one to stare at her, up at the posters, then back at her.

"I was a pin-up, not a centerfold," Louise amended.

Luc groaned.

Tee-John laughed.

"Lemme see," Charmaine said, pushing her way forward. Then, examining the two posters in questions, she remarked, "Wow! You were a real beauty, auntie. Bet I could do one of these pin-up pictures. What do you think, Rusty?"

Rusty just made a gurgling sound.

"All of those pin-up artists made the women look like they had perfect figures, almost too perfect. There probably isn't a female alive with breasts so perky and waists so small. It was almost misogynistic and sexist, really. Worse than Barbie dolls," Celine informed them all.

Did I mention Celine is a know-it-all, bless her heart?

"Bull-pucky!" Louise countered.

"Get out of there," Celine hissed as Etienne moved farther inside the tent, getting an eyeful of what would certainly appeal to an adolescent boy. To men, too, truth to tell. "Women don't really look like that," she continued to instruct her son. "It's just a male fantasy."

"God bless fantasies," Tee-John murmured as his eyes swept the array of posters.

Celine glared at him.

He waggled his eyebrows at her. "Hey, darlin', if I buy you one of those garter belts being sold back there with a pair of seamed stockings, I could take your picture with my cell phone, and—"

"Grow up!" Celine said.

"Never!" Tee-John and Louise hooted at the same time.

Celine had to smile then, shaking her head at the two of them.

Then Tee-John put his arm around his wife's shoulders and tugged her closer to his side, kissing the top of her head. She could hear him whisper, "You look better than any of these models, babe."

What a charmer!"

What's the difference," Etienne asked Louise, "between a centerfold and a pin-up?"

"The difference is clothes," Tante Lulu explained, following after Etienne. There was nothing but LeDeuxs in the big tent now. "Pin-ups wore clothes, centerfolds were buck nekkid. Mostly." She was peering closely at the two posters in question. She remembered when she'd had them done. Originally, she'd just wanted a racy picture to give to her fiancé, Phillipe Prudhomme, before he went away, but the painter, an associate of Vargas, Emmanuel Delgado, had convinced her to do several others, which had been used in a series of pin-up calendars sold in military canteens around the world.

One of the posters showed Louise wearing a red silk robe that exposed one leg up to the thigh and a cleavage no real woman ever had; in it, she posed on a pink chaise lounge, with her back arched so that her long, dark hair, like Charmaine's Veronica Lake 'do, hung back almost to the floor. Her hair hadn't been that long, either. Another bit of artistic license. On the other poster, she wore a strapless white bathing suit and white high-heeled pumps, posed against a boat. Perched on her up-do hairstyle, ala Judy Garland or Joan Crawford, was a white sailor cap.

"I looked good, dint I?" she said to Tee-John.

"Damn good! You actually appear tall in that one. At least five-seven, or –eight."

"Oh, that was a trick all the pin-up painters did at that time. They wanted tall women, of course, but they had ways ta make us shorter ladies have longer legs. Like that picture shopping they do t'day."

"She means photoshopping," Celine told Tee-John.

"I know what it means," Louise snapped.

The owner of the tent, overhearing their conversation, came up to them and asked Louise, "Would you mind autographing a few of your posters?"

"Sure," she said.

Actually, her family members bought most of them, wanting evidence, no doubt, that their outrageous Tante Lulu had been outrageous, even back then.

"What do you say to a little lunch?" Luc suggested. "There's a food tent over there. Aunt Hattie's Tea Room. Looks like fun. Scones with clotted cream and lemon curd. Crustless finger sandwiches. Yum."

She didn't know if Luc was serious or poking fun. Whatever. Louise wasn't really hungry, but she'd been on her feet all morning, and she'd welcome a little break.

They had to pass the USO tent before they got to the tea room.

Sylvie linked arms with her on one side and Luc on the other. "Did you ever go to one of these?" Sylvie asked her.

"Are ya kiddin'? I lived in those canteens durin' the war. It's where I first met Phillipe. Well, not really 'met' fer the first time. We knew each other from down the bayou when we were both young'uns, but Phillipe was six years older than me. It was in the Nawleans USO where we got t'gether—really got t'gether, if ya get my meanin'."

"We got your meanin', auntie. No explanation needed," Luc said.

"Are ya funnin' me again?"

"Me?" He looked at her with mock innocence.

"Fool!" she said and glanced toward the USO tent as they passed.

Then stopped dead in her tracks and did a double take.

Disengaging herself from Luc and Sylvie, she moved hesitantly into the tent where many pictures of USOs from Louisiana were displayed. It was the black-and-white photo, enlarged to poster size, which showed her and Phillipe slow-dancing at the Fort Polk USO New Year's Eve dance in 1943.

Phillipe hadn't been overly tall. Only about five foot ten, but with her high-heeled pumps and dancing on her tippy toes, there had only been a few inches difference in their height. She, wearing her then-favorite tea-length gown of red chiffon, was gazing up at him with adoration. He, in his Navy dress uniform, Cajun to the core, was smiling down at her. A couple in love, no doubt about it.

Louise remembered that night as if it were yesterday. The band had been playing "Star Dust." She could still smell his Aqua Velva, and her own musky Tabu. Still feel his nighttime stubble against her cheek. The press of his one hand against her lower back, the other hand holding her palm against his heart, thus displaying her new engagement ring, which had been a Christmas present. The whisper of his "I love you, *chère*" against her ear.

That's when all the events of the day, the nostalgia, the jarred memories, good and so painful they still made her heart hurt in her chest, took their toll. There was only so much a lady could take.

Louise, for only the second time in her life, fell into a dead faint.

CHAPTER 1

1942

Begin the Beguine...

"Son of a gun!" Lt. Phillipe Prudhomme exclaimed the instant that he saw Louise Rivard in the white clingy dress and the strappy high heels, dancing her pretty little ass off at the USO in New Orleans. Sure as bayou mud stinks, he was a goner. Big trouble incoming!

He had dated Louise a few times the summer following his graduation as an ensign from the Naval Academy four years ago, prior to his entering medical school. But it had been nothing serious. His relationships with women never were. How could they be? In many ways, he was married to Uncle Sam, who owned his sorry ass for the next ten or more years.

A small price to pay for a free education, he

supposed. Hell, it was the only way a poor bayou boy would have ever been able to afford college, especially during the Depression. And he had to be grateful for the rare exemption he'd been given to postpone his active duty commitment in order to complete medical school first.

In any case, Louise had only been sixteen at the time. A kid.

Now, thanks to Pearl Harbor, Phillipe had put his medical career plans on hold after only two years of med school, and gone active. And Louise Rivard was no longer a child. *Mon Dieu*, was that an understatement! There must be something in the bayou air to bring about this transformation. Or else, he'd been blind four years ago.

His pawpaw had warned him that this would happen one day. "Ya think yer immune, boy. Ya think plannin' yer life out is cut and dry, like love will fit inta yer schedule. But wait and see. It happens ta all the Prudhomme men in our family. We call it the Prudhomme Whammy. You'll be walkin' along, free and easy, and wham bam! There'll she be. The one! And yer free 'n easy days'll be over. Guar-an-teed! It happened ta me when I was only seventeen. Dint happen ta yer Uncle James till he was forty-six. It comes when it comes. And it ain't jist the pretty gals that do the trick, either. Mah second cousin, Louis, fell lak a rock when he first saw Mabel, and she's homely as a mud hen, bless her heart."

Phillipe had laughed at the time. What young man believed an old geezer like his grandfather had any wisdom about modern times, or about Phillipe in particular since he was different from everyone in his Cajun family? They told him so all the time.

Could the old man possibly be right? Phillipe was for damn sure standing in the middle of the crowded social club, gawking at the girl like a swabbie on his first ship, when, in fact, he was a twenty-six-year-old lieutenant junior grade officer whose Naval Academy nickname had been Prudie, and not just because of his surname. Phillipe had maintained an almost prudish attitude toward women in his single-minded quest to succeed, requiring focus, focus, focus.

Focus be damned at the moment. His heart was beating so fast, he could scarcely breathe, and every fine hair on his body stood at attention. A certain part might even salute if he wasn't careful.

"Hubba hubba! Who's the dish?" Petty Officer Franklin Mitchell asked, elbowing Phillipe in the ribs to get his attention. Mitch, a Yankee from Boston, had latched onto Phillipe like a shrimp boat barnacle ever since they'd left the Bourbon Street wedding reception an hour ago for their buddy, Beauregard Breaux. Yeah, Bo Bro. Corny as only a Southern name could be. The three of them would be part of the new S & R unit, Amphibious Scouts and Raiders, being formed shortly in Little Creek, Virginia. Frogmen.

He never would have stopped at the USO if not for Mitch's urging. Not his thing. Besides, the male/female ratio was at least ten to one.

"It's Louise Rivard from down Bayou Black," Phillipe replied to Mitch's question.

"You know her?"

Mitch's surprise was kind of insulting. Phillipe hadn't been *that* celibate...aka, focused. But maybe he meant that Phillipe was known to be kind of stiff in his mannerisms, not usually a magnet for hot women. And Louise was hot! "I don't *know her* know her," he said, not about to disclose his few past "dates." Such revelation would only make him seem even more of a knucklehead. "She's about six years younger than me. I went to the academy right after high school, and she was probably still in elementary school then." *And she looked nothing like this sultry siren when I was back here four years ago.*

As he watched (Mitch having gone off to find his own dancing partner), Louise jitterbugged with one soldier after another to songs like "Chattanooga Choo-Choo," "Boogie Woogie Bugle Boy," and "Alexander's Ragtime Band." She was a really good dancer, never missing a beat as her partners swung her out, twirled her around and back into a near-embrace, even dipped occasionally, so low her long hair brushed the floor. Once he even saw her garter belt. The whole time, she smiled and chatted up the besotted guys who clearly lusted after her.

Like me.

She used her hands and her arms expressively as she danced. In fact, all parts of her body parts moved to the beat. Not in an overtly sexual way, but sensual. And graceful. Sensual grace. Hah! That was a new way of saying Hot Broad.

At one point, she noticed him staring at her, and their eyes connected. Even then, she didn't trip or mess up her dance steps. But she was aware of him after that, he could tell.

Of course, it could be because he was wearing summer dress whites, a request of Beau's bride for her formal wedding. His uniform stood out in this sea of khaki. Oh, there were Navy guys in white here, too, from the NAS, but they wore the typical sailor uniforms with Dixie Cup covers in their hands, or stuffed in back pockets. Mostly, the service men crowding this USO were Army from Camp Polk or Camp Beauregard, or guys home on leave from other posts. Not that Polk didn't have its own USO up at DeRidder, but the rumors of sin to be had in New Orleans were a constant lure to horny soldiers, even in such innocent surroundings as these USOs where the hostesses were supposed to be "good girls."

In the break between songs, Mitch came back, towing a pretty blonde in hand, and said, "We're going out for a soda." Code word for necking...or something more. "You gonna make your move or what?"

Yeah, he probably was. This attraction was too strong to be ignored.

And that was saying a lot because, up to now, Phillipe would have walked away from this kind of temptation. No excessive drinking when on liberty, like some of his Navy buddies were inclined to indulge (there was a lot to forget about with that war in Europe calling their names). No gambling (who could afford to lose even a tenner when half his paycheck was sent home to his parents?). No cigarettes (ever liked the taste, and expensive). No brothels (that money issue, again, plus the risk of diseases, as graphically explained to every first-year plebe or swabbie. Can anyone say Cupid's Itch?). And definitely no serious relationships with women (he'd never had a steady girlfriend—ever—which was probably why he'd had no real interest in Louise back then).

If that made him a cold fish, or a knucklehead, so be it! Phillipe was determined to rise above the poverty of his bayou upbringing and become "somebody." Hopefully, a physician, God willing and the war not lasting too long.

With nothing going for him other than a brighter than usual brain, he'd been pounded around quite a bit. Four years as a midshipman at the Naval Academy in Maryland (which was Yankee land to this Southern boy, no matter what anyone said about some friggin' Mason-Dixon line), four summer cruises on the USS Yorktown (where he got mocked for his "redneck" drawl and learned to give as good as he got), and two years of medical school before he made lieutenant junior grade bars on re-entry to active duty.

And he'd done damn well so far. But he was a long way from his ultimate goal, and that would require single-minded dedication. His life at the moment had no room for a woman, other than a quick raking of the coals here and there, and definitely not this tempting bit of bayou fluff, who could easily drag him back to his Cajun roots.

Still, Louise was a sight to behold. A sexy little thing, no more than five-two or five-three, before donning those lay-me-down red high heels with straps that tied into bows at her trim ankles. He would be dreaming about those shoes tonight, for sure.

Bet I could untie those knots with my teeth.

Small she might be, but perfectly proportioned. Oh, man, was she built! Breasts which were small but appeared large, because of her petite frame. A tiny waist tapering out to curvy hips and what appeared to be a... please, God!...heart-shaped ass. A pint-sized Betty Grable.

She wore a short-sleeved, knee-length, red-belted, white dress of some clingy material that hugged her upper body and hips, then swirled out as she danced. Caramel-colored Cajun eyes expressed her every emotion, mostly flirty laughter, and dark hair hanging down to her shoulders in waves whipped this way and that as she danced.

Like a butterfly she was, mesmerizing to all those who watched her with fascination. Colorful. Carefree. Daring the observer to catch her if they could.

Enough!

As the music changed suddenly to a much slower, "As Time Goes By," he forged forward, making a path through the crowd. Without asking, he held out a hand to her, ignoring the Army grunt who'd expected to be her partner.

Louise tilted her head to the side at his nerve, but stepped into his arms. He was only five-ten, and her high heels brought her up to just the right height. With her left hand on his shoulder and her right hand in his, there was still ample space between them. To him, it felt like the most intimate embrace.

"Louise," he said as they swayed together. That's all. Just her name. In a husky fool voice. Smoldering, that's how his fellow midshipmen at the Academy used to describe a certain voice, or look, and practice it in front of a mirror, himself included. Looking for charm in all the wrong places. Total drips, that's what they'd been. Apparently, he still was.

She arched her brows. "Phillipe Prudhomme, I do declare. I thought you had become a Yankee and abandoned us poor Southern gals for some snooty Yankee dame."

"Darlin', there's nothin' up north to compare with a Southern belle, especially a Cajun one," he drawled. *Yep, drip, drip, drip. First I smolder, then I drawl. Next, I'll be drooling. And, jeesh! I thought I lost my Southern accent.* "With all the service men crowdin' you, I'm surprised you even recognized me."

She grinned at his teasing. "Darlin'," she said, copying him, "I've known you since ya wrestled a gator on Bayou Black and claimed ta be Tarzan, king of the bayou jungle. How could I ever forget you?"

"I was twelve years old, and it was a baby gator." He laughed. "And how could I ever forget the barefoot Cajun girl with a sunburnt nose whose claim to fame was that she could catch crawfish by dipping her big toe in bayou mud and letting the critters hang on?"

She blushed at that memory, but then she added with a saucy wink, "I still can, but those mudbug claws ruin mah toenail polish."

"*Comment ca va, chère?*" he asked, reverting to Cajun French, asking how she was doing.

She shrugged. "*Comme ci, comme ca, cher.*" So-so.

He loved this banter with its Cajun undertones. It felt kind of like coming home.

"What are you doin' here in Nawleans? I thought you were up north, studyin' ta be a doctor or somethin'."

"I was. I am. I mean, I started my studies at the Naval Academy, and was lucky enough to be able to postpone my military commitment after graduation until after I complete medical school. I got in two years, but then the war interrupted and I'm back on active." He shrugged after his overlong explanation. All she'd probably wanted was a simple "I am."

She nodded, though, as if understanding. Lots of people's plans had been put on hold by the damn war. "So, you're not actually a doctor yet?"

"*Mais non.* Far from it."

"And you're back here...why?"

"I'm on liberty for two weeks, and was in my buddy's wedding down the street tonight. Otherwise, I wouldn't be wearing this ice-cream-man outfit," he said, waving a hand in front of himself to explain his more formal attire.

"You look good in that uniform, Phillipe. *Trés* handsome!"

He'd been feeling foolish up to now, overdressed, like he stood out, and not in a good way. Her compliment made him feel good until she added, "Tsk, tsk! You men and your uniforms! It's not fair to us poor females who are dazzled by all that handsomeness." She fanned her face with a hand and blew out a little breath, as if overheated.

He grinned and shook his head with wonder. Females didn't react to him that way. Not ones as attractive as Louise. His eyes swept over her again, taking in her amazing appearance. "You...are...a...doll," he murmured, before he had a chance to bite his tongue.

"And that surprises you?"

"Actually, it does. How come I never noticed you before...that way?"

"The wrong time," she conjectured.

She was probably right. "So, what are you doing here, Miss Louise Marie Rivard of crawdad-catching fame? Nawleans is a long way from Bayou Black." Well, it was less than an hour away, by car, but Cajun girls usually stuck close to home. Or they used to.

"I work here. At Higgins Industries."

"Where they build the Liberty Ships?"

She nodded.

"You work on the line?" Lots of women, even ones who'd never worked before, were filling the assembly lines of factories these days while their men went off to war.

She shook her head. "I'm a typist. Been there for two years, since I graduated from high school."

"I always thought you'd become a *traiteur*, like your mother and grandmother."

"I would have. I might still one day. Folk healin' is passed on through some females in my family, but the money here in the city is too good ta pass up."

He would bet she sent money home, like he did. Cajuns were hard-working people, but most of them were poor, struggling to support large families on blue-collar salaries. "Yeah, the war changes everything."

They were carrying on this conversation as they slow-danced, but it was hard to hear with the loud music and the conversations and laughter around them.

"I hafta leave soon," she told him during a pause in the music, "if I wanna catch the last streetcar home."

"A streetcar? I assumed that you lived at home on the bayou and traveled into the city."

"It's too hard to travel back and forth every day, even if I was able to get the gas rations. I share a cottage on Rampart Street with three other girls."

"The old *plaçage* district?" he asked with a grin. Years ago, back in the 1700s and 1800s, white, upper-class Louisiana men had maintained their quadroon mistresses in a recognized legal system called *plaçage*. In New Orleans, Rampart Street became known for its *placée* cottages, easily identifiable by their vivid colors.

"Yes, but it's quite respectable t'day. Well, maybe a little shady," she admitted, and grinned. Obviously, there was still some wild in this bayou girl, who liked pushing the edge.

That settled it. "I'll drive you home." But then he thought of something. "You going steady with anyone, *chère?*"

"A little late for askin' that, isn't it?" she asked. "No, I'm not seein' anyone reg'lar."

He squeezed her hand, the message being, *Until now*. Everything was happening fast and hard, but for once in his life, he couldn't care.

Without further words, he led her off the dance floor. Along the way, he told Mitch he'd see him back at the hotel room they shared, where the wedding reception had been held. After tonight, Phillipe would be staying at his parent's home or over at the NSA officer quarters, and Mitch would be headed north to his home, where he had a fiancée waiting for him.

Phillipe laced his fingers with hers as they walked, and for a while neither of them spoke. He was overwhelmed with the emotions that washed over him, filling him.

And they hadn't even kissed yet.

She laughed when she saw his car...a fifteen-year-old Triumph roadster that had seen better days even when he'd bought it as an abandoned wreck when he was sixteen years old. "You're still drivin' this rust bucket?"

"Hey, be careful you don't insult Belle. She gets me where I want to go."

"You call your car Belle? What is it about men and the female names they give their precious cars?"

And precious body parts, too, truth to tell. Names, that is. Not female names. "She's pretty, and temperamental, but when her motor is running, she—"

"Enough! I get the picture." Louise laughed again.

He loved the sound of her laughter. In these uncertain times, any laughter was a lift to a soldier's spirits, but her laugh...it was something else. Light. Flirty. Teasing. Like Louise herself.

Phillipe pulled up in front of the rundown yellow cottage with blue shutters. This street was just outside the red light district, but like Louise had said, respectable. Though barely. Her daddy would have a fit if he knew where she was living.

He didn't bother to ask if he could come in, figuring her roommates would be around; all the lights were lit in the cottage windows. So, they sat in his car and talked, and talked. Not about the war, what action he'd seen, how long the war would last, about the good news coming out that day of an American victory in Guadal-canal, or the increasingly horrendous news seeping out of Germany about what the Nazis were doing to the Jews in concentration camps. Instead, he told her about his plans for the future...both immediate in S & R and long-term in medicine.

"Wouldn't a medic be more in line with your career plans?" she asked.

"Yes, but I like the idea of being in on a new venture like S & R. Besides, I need a break from medicine. Not that a man with some medical experience won't be helpful in the small teams that operate out in enemy territory on their own."

She shrugged, obviously not really understanding the male yen for adventure. Then she told him all the inter-esting stuff she'd learned about folk healing from her mother and grandmother, and how she eventually expected to take over the business.

He marveled at the uses made of native herbs and animal parts, and laughed at some of them. Like gator teeth or egret feathers or snake skins in natural remedies. And the dangerous expeditions Louise had made into the swamps to gather herbs with her mother and aging mawmaw.

"And you wouldn't believe what I can do with love potions," she told him, batting her eyelashes seductively.

"Should I be worried?" He laughed.

"I joke about some of the weird potions, but, really, Phillipe, the folk remedies passed down for generations are often as good, or better, than modern medicine."

"I'm not arguing with that." He put up his hands in surrender. "Odd, but I can see how the two could work together...my practicing professional medicine and your folk medicine."

"You say that like we have a future together," she remarked, but not with any surprise. She had to be aware of this "thing" blooming between them.

And they hadn't even kissed yet.

"Would that be so hard to believe?" he asked, putting his arm over the back of her seat and stroking a swath of her hair which had a tendency to curl around his finger.

She shook her head. "I knew back four years ago, but you were such a clunkerhead when it came ta seein' me as more'n a chile."

He tipped her chin toward him so that he could see her face more directly. "You knew what, darlin'?"

"That we would be together some day." She made that bold statement with such surety that he couldn't help but feel she knew something he'd been too dull to understand. A clunkerhead, for sure.

He thought about telling her how impossible it would be for them to have a future together. First of all, there was the war. Then the years left of medical school, followed by even more years in the military as a physician before he could ever contemplate a private practice. Sure, some military men married...in fact, lots of them were rushing to get hitched before they shipped out...but Louise was a Cajun girl. He couldn't see her being a Navy wife, moving from post to post, far from any bayou.

Holy-hot-damn-hell! Marriage? Am I crazy? We haven't even kissed yet, and I'm planning the wedding.

But then he kissed her.

And that ended all questions.

He was in love. No question about it. In an instant. No choice. Bam! Just like PawPaw had predicted. There was no reason involved...the logistics of war separation, the impossibility of a Cajun girl living up north or across the ocean, his need to focus on his medical career. None of that mattered in this burst of insanity.

This was bad, bad, bad.

No, this was good, good, good.

And then she kissed him back, her sweet lips telling him more than words that they were meant for each other. The future be damned! In this moment, despite all the obstacles, anything was possible.

CHAPTER 2

Accentuate the positive...

he next day, Louise was in the passenger seat of Phillipe's decrepit roadster, cruising along the one-lane road leading to her family's cottage on Bayou Black. It was barely ten a.m., but already the late April air was warm and humid, promising a hot Louisiana day of at least eighty degrees.

With the top down on Phillipe's sports car (which was a stretch for this rattletrap if sports car denoted luxury), she took a deep breath of the bayou air. She smelled wild magnolia and swamp mud, dew on wet grass, and slow-moving water, but more than that. She recognized the mixture of scents for what it was. Home.

There was an added dimension to her pleasure today —Phillipe. With him sitting beside her, taking her hand when it was free from the gear shift, the emotional impact was almost too much. And yet not enough.

41

She was so happy, she couldn't stop grinning, occasionally letting loose with laughter at nothing in particular. In fact, she was practically jumping in her seat with excitement.

"Are you always so happy?" Phillipe asked when he slowed down behind a tractor. "You're like a giddy butterfly, fluttering about, spreading your *joie de vivre*."

"Is joy of life a bad thing?"

"Not at all. In fact, you're a breath of fresh air in a dreary world." He grimaced. "Could I sound any more sappy? Can you tell how uncool I am?"

If he only knew how uncool she found him! More like hot, hot, hot. As for "a dreary world," he must mean the war. Instead of bringing up that subject, she accused him, "A poet now. Be still my heart."

He chucked her under the chin in reprimand for her teasing. "I read that line in a greeting card, except it was a pretty butterfly, not giddy, and instead of *joie de vivre*, it was sunshine."

"You don't need fancy words to woo me over."

"What? You're already wooed?"

"Uh-huh."

"You shouldn't tell me that."

"Why?"

"It gives me ideas."

"I like ideas." She could tell that she disconcerted him with her racy words. Good! Phillipe was too stiff and serious by nature, always had been. He needed shaking up.

"I just wondered if you're always so happy, or is it

just being with me?" he asked, attempting to steer the conversation in his own direction.

"Oh, you, definitely," she said with a smile.

Phillipe returned her smile.

The farmer veered his tractor off the road onto a lane leading inland toward a barn, and Phillipe shifted gears to a higher speed. Conversation was almost impossible in the open car with the roar of the engine and the wind. But they didn't need to talk. This unspoken something between them was a blossoming swamp flower. Wonderful and scary at the same time. Too precious to dissect for fear of it wilting before it had a chance to bloom.

Now she was the one turning into a corny poet. But she noticed Phillipe following her suit in inhaling the unique bayou air, like he was storing up memories. When they slowed down once again, this time for an alligator crossing the road, she remarked, "It's true what they say. You can take the man out of the bayou, but you can't take the bayou out of the man."

He squeezed her hand. "Or the woman."

"*Mais oui,*" she replied. "Especially if they are of the born and bred Cajun persuasion. I might have flown the coop, working and living in Nawleans the past two years," *working out my Cajun wild, according to my mother,* "but it's this stretch of Bayou Black that I still call home. And not just because Mama and Papa are here, holding down the roost."

"I get it. Your roots are here, firmly planted in this little stretch of heaven...Bayou Black." A sadness suddenly filled his face which surprised her, but then he added, "You could never live anywhere but here, or close by, could you?"

Ah! Now she understood. He was wondering if she'd ever be able to live up north, or wherever the military sent him. With him? Oh, there was a question! With him, she was pretty sure she could live in Alaska, or some Amazon jungle, maybe even California. But those were questions and answers to be dealt with later. Today, she wanted to bask in this first day of their new life. And that's exactly how it felt. No longer her life. Now, it was their life. "Don't be too sure about that, Phillipe."

The gator finally crossed the road and ambled toward the bayou stream, and Phillipe gunned the engine and shifted gears again so they could go faster. She inhaled deeply, and had to admit, she would miss all this. Even as she worked and lived in the city, she had to come back often for her bayou fix, especially this time of the year. Spring was her favorite season, but springtime on the bayou was especially wonderful with its almost overpowering assault on the senses. The smells, the sounds, and the sights overwhelmed some folks, but not her. And they were ever-changing as new animals were born, new plants budded, new bayou streams rose up out of nowhere. Always something new. At the same time, the bayou stayed the same. Ancient live oak and bald cypress trees had probably been here in prehistoric times.

Not so ancient were the Burma Shave signs spaced far apart along the road that drew a smile. They'd been changed since she was here last month.

If hugging
On highways
Is your sport
Trade in your car
For a davenport
Burma Shave

She and Phillipe exchanged smiles. "Do they have these signs up north, too?"

"Oh, yeah! My favorite is: "Let's make Hitler, And Hirohito, Look as sick as, Old Benito.""

"I know another war one. My roommate saw it when she was in Baton Rouge. 'With glamour girls, you'll never click, Bewhiskered like a, Bolshevik.'"

"Lots of guys grow beards."

"Oh, don't grow a beard. You're so handsome clean-shaven."

"I'll never have a beard then," he promised and gave her a wink, which made her insides feel sort of quivery.

As they traveled along the familiar road, there was little traffic, but when there was, one vehicle had to pull off to the berm, which was what Phillipe did now, letting Jake Hebert pass them in his milk truck. Jake waved at her and saluted Phillipe, even though Phillipe was out of uniform. Today, Phillipe wore a white button shirt, open at the neck with the sleeves rolled up and tucked into tan, pleated slacks, with suspenders (for effect, mostly, he didn't have any fear of losing his pants), scruffy old canvas boat shoes, and a straw fedora. He could have been wearing bib overalls, like her daddy did on the shrimp boats, and she would have still considered him the handsomest man around.

Beulah Mae Petit, sweeping the front stoop of Boudreaux's General Store, yelled out, "Welcome home!" Louise wasn't sure if the welcome was intended for her or Phillipe.

And then a truckload of soldiers from Fort Polk, who'd probably been out on some kind of early morning maneuvers, approached, and Phillipe pulled well off the road to give them room. The soldiers whistled and waved, definitely aiming their regards at her. Fort Polk was some distance away, but with the war in Europe and the new Selective Service Act, thousands of boys were being drafted every day. Then, too, the training grounds of the Military Maneuvers operation in Louisiana, started two years ago, were often moved off base to environments like the bayou which facsimililated some jungle habitats in the Pacific where they might be sent to fight. Like that Guadalcanal place.

Finally, Phillipe pulled onto the crushed-shell driveway on the side of her family's cottage, which had been built years ago in the old Cajun style of bousillage— fuzzy mud mixed with Spanish moss and pulverized clam shells. The Cajuns, or Acadians, who'd been exiled to this new land in the 1700s were ever the survivors. Didn't matter that the land was swampy or that they'd have to subsist on animals no one else would eat, like possum, or squirrel, or even gators. Or build their homes of mud.

It was a humble, two-bedroom house, but neat, with a stretch of lawn in back leading to the narrow bayou stream. Sitting dead center in the yard was a young fig tree which might begin bearing fruit for the first time this year, just in time for her mother's famous jelly. Usually, her mother bought the fruit by the bushel from the French Quarter Market on one of their periodic treks to New Orleans, but then her father, Samuel Rivard, had given a fig plant to her mother three years ago for their thirtieth anniversary on condition that she would make her Figgy Cake with Buttermilk Glaze on every special occasion. As if her mother didn't already!

Yes, it would be hard to live somewhere else, Louise realized, but then she glanced at Phillipe, seeing the sad understanding in his eyes. "It doesn't change anything," she whispered.

He looked skeptical.

And, of course, there was a vegetable patch off to the side. Forget about the Victory Gardens that President Roosevelt urged patriotic Americans to plant. Cajuns already knew about subsistence gardening. And in this sub-tropical climate, everything flourished...okra, string beans, peas, carrots, radishes, peppers, tomatoes, potatoes, melons, garlic, cabbages, celery. You name it, they grew it.

It being springtime, the garden had been recently tilled and seeded, but the only things showing were fall-planted kale and Swiss chard, and early onions and lettuce. Her mother was out there now with a hoe in hand, which she was using to loosen the soil between the rows. But then she suddenly used the hoe to lift a garden snake out of her way. She didn't kill it because garden snakes were mostly harmless and actually beneficial, eating some of the pesky insects and slugs.

The engine idled as Phillipe took in the setting, which was pretty much like his parents' place up the bayou a few miles. "I'll pick you up in a few hours, *chère*, and we can spend the rest of the day together. Maybe drive up to Lake Pontchartrain?"

She nodded, a bit distracted by his fingers which were laced with hers now, the thumb stroking her wrist. Could he feel how fast her heart was beating? Did he hate being apart for even these few hours, like she did? "I could bring a picnic basket."

He looked at her like she was the only food he needed. More stroking, and that look in his eyes. Hungry, it was.

But she didn't have any time for these thoughts because her mother had turned and was shading her eyes from the already bright sun before recognizing her.

"Louisey! I dint expect you so early," Mama exclaimed, using the nickname she'd been given long ago by her older brother Frank who'd been eleven years old when Louise, the unexpected "oops" baby, had been born. Putting down the hoe, she left the garden area and walked toward Louise, a welcome smile on her face, soon replaced by confusion as her glance hit on Phillipe. Suddenly, the smile returned. "Phillipe Prudhomme, is that you, boy? I hardly recognized you. Las' time I saw you was at the Crawfish Boil in Lafayette when yer pawpaw won the zydeco contest."

"Mrs. Rivard! I remember that day. I was thirteen years old then. PawPaw put away his washboard long ago. In fact, he played the *frottoir* only when he was drunk, and MawMaw insisted he give it up or she would burn the thing."

Her mother laughed, knowing the truth of what Phillipe said. The bayou was a small community with no secrets.

Alma Rivard looked like so many Cajun housewives of certain years. Her hair was pulled back into a soft bun at her nape. Despite the gray threads in her brown hair, her face was unlined and glowed with a healthy tan from working outdoors. She wore a mid-calf, faded housedress that buttoned up the front and might once have been red and white gingham, but was now a faded rose. Her legs were bare, leading down to rubber boots that accommodated her gardening, as well as forays into the swamps for the precious roots and herbs that she used in her *traiteur*, or folk-healing, practice.

Was Phillipe wondering if this was how Louise would look when she was older? If so, he didn't seem displeased. Instead, he laughed and got out of the car, going up to her mother to give her a kiss on both cheeks.

After exchanging pleasantries, Phillipe declined an offer to come inside for sweet tea, saying that his mother was expecting him for lunch, and his father would want more tall tales of his military feats, and his grandfather likely had the fishing poles baited and ready to drop into

49

the nearest bayou stream. He soon left, promising to be back in three hours.

Louise's mother was sure to have lots of questions about Phillipe, especially since Louise had never brought a young man home before, and especially with the good-bye kiss Phillipe had dropped on her lips. But she had other issues first.

"Lord help me!" Her mother made the sign of the cross when she took in Louise's attire, especially the pants. Trousers on ladies were still a rarity here on the bayou—scandalous, really. Women her mama's age considered them suitable only for horseback riding or work on a factory assembly line. Even then, only loose women would dare expose their bodies like that.

Louise's pants were far from tight, but they were red, made of a silky blend. A white blouse with shoulder pads and three buttons undone for cleavage (not that she had much of that, despite her padded bra) was tucked into the high waistband, accentuating her figure. White wedgie sandals gave her added height, along with her upswept hairdo which had been kept mostly in place with a scarf while they'd been riding in the open air.

Her crimson lip color would also be a red flag to her mother, who believed red shoes and red lips were an advertisement for prostitutes. In fact, she claimed that red shoes were a signal that a woman wasn't wearing any underpants. Where she'd got that idea, Louise had no idea. Probably from the spicy detective paperbacks her father read and hid under their mattress, as if they were something forbidden. Good thing Louise wasn't wearing her red high heels today, but then, the trousers and red lips were enough of a shocker.

Her mother shook her head with dismay. "Wild! You allus was a wild chile, and it appears nothin' has changed. Why you gotta dress lak a loose lady?"

Louise barely stifled a laugh. "Oh, Mama, loose ladies don't dress like this. In fact, I've never seen a prostitute in slacks strolling Bourbon Street."

"For shame! To even speak of such! I swear, you mus' have wildness in yer blood from yer father's side of the fam'ly. It certainly dint come from my kin. Talk about!"

It was true. Louise had always been a wild child, a fey, barefooted sprite running through the swamps and coffee-colored streams of Bayou Black. And she was a wild woman now, but only in the sense she was a free spirit. Yes, she liked fancy clothes, dancing, and the occasional hard liquor. No one could toss back an Oyster Shooter, or two, like Louise, and still shimmy till dawn. Then get up for work.

But not wild in the promiscuous or immoral sense. In fact, at twenty years of age, more than few people would be surprised to learn she was still a virgin.

Louise loved giving the wrong impression.

But she loved her mother and didn't want to hurt her. Reaching out, she pulled her mother into a tight hug and said, "Oh, Mama, not ta worry! I'm still a good girl."

Her mother understood what she meant without spelling it out. She made a clucking sound and said, "'Course ya are. I never thought otherwise. Still...must ya dress so scandalous?" But then, her mother grinned and said, "On the other hand, pants would come in handy fer gardenin' and trampin' through the swamp. Do they come in my size?"

Louise knew suddenly what she would be getting her mother for Christmas this year.

As they walked arm and arm toward the back door, her mother said, "So, what's with Phillipe?"

"I think I'm in love, Mama."

"Oh, Lord!"

"What? You don't like Phillipe?"

"I like him fine, but I suspect my 'good girl' is about ta be tested."

Guar-an-teed!

CHAPTER 3

Getting to know you…

They spent a leisurely afternoon by the lake, talking, kissing, laughing, looking at each other with wonder. It was the best day of Phillipe's life. So far.

Louise had brought everything they needed for a picnic in a large basket that barely fit in the trunk of his car. A tablecloth, plates, and silverware that she'd have to return to her mother, and seemingly everything she could find in the cottage icebox. Thin slices of cold chicken, cooked boudin sausage, crawfish salad, beans and rice, leftover fried green tomatoes, charred okra, and spicy pickles. All of it heavy on the Tabasco, also known as Cajun lightning. Phillipe had learned while up north that Louisiana was as famous for inventing the hot sauce, as if it was for its beignets, pralines, and gumbo. Louise

53

had also packed buttered biscuits, a Southern tradition, and some kind of glazed cake made with figs and buttermilk. Two Mason jars of sweet tea chilled in the rocks at the water's edge.

But the food was incidental to this picnic.

They half reclined on the blanket, watching some boaters paddling by in the distance. He trailed a fingertip over her arm, from the edge of her short sleeve, slowly down to her wrist, and saw the fine hairs raise on her arm in reaction.

His male ego rose about three notches, knowing he could affect her so. His gaze moved upward to see that her lips were parted and her eyelashes fluttering.

Arousal?

Oh, boy!

Another two notches.

"You're staring, Phillipe," she said, not for the first time today.

"I know," he replied and continued to stare. "You are so beautiful."

She crinkled her nose at him.

He loved the way she crinkled her nose.

"You probably say that to all the girls. I know I'm not beautiful. I'm too short, and my mouth is too big for my face, and Mama says I'm too wild."

"Number one, there are no other girls. Two, you're just the right size for me. And three, you have to know how much I like your mouth. As for four, I can't wait to find out if your mother's right." He waggled his eyebrows at her.

"Oh, you!" She tried to swat at him, but he grabbed for her, pulling her down to her back on the blanket so they could neck some more. After a while, they walked barefooted along the lake, holding hands, sometimes not talking, just enjoying being with each other, other times with her chattering away about anything and everything. He'd had to talk her into taking off her shoes. She hated being so short. He told her, "The best things come in small packages."

"Another line?"

"Maybe," he said, but truly, he didn't mind her being almost eight inches shorter than him. It made him feel oddly protective of her in a masculine sense.

"I have to leave in four days," he told her suddenly, having put off the announcement long enough, not wanting to spoil their day.

She stopped, forcing him to stop, too. They still held hands, her left in his right. She put her right palm on his chest, right over his heart, and looked up at him, a mixture of anger and fear in her pretty brown eyes.

"What do you mean? I thought you had a two-week liberty."

He nodded, taking her free hand and kissing the knuckles. "I did have a longer leave, but I got a call at the base this morning. We...the S & R team...need to be back in Little Creek, Virginia by Thursday at oh eight hundred. That's eight a.m."

"Oh, Phillipe! So little time!"

He resumed walking, still holding her hand. "Let's spend all the time together that we can. And that won't be the end, darlin', I promise. We'll write. I'll come back whenever I can, and maybe you can even come see me." He was talking too much and too fast. A clear sign he was nervous, which had to be obvious to her. Did she wonder why? He wondered himself. Was he nervous about leaving her? The war? Dangers he might be facing? How to handle good-byes? Hah! Those were nothing compared to what really ailed him: How, or if, he should tell her that he loved her, without making any promises.

He didn't care what thousands of other dumb soldiers did. He wasn't going to take the chance of marriage, leaving a grieving widow behind. Maybe later, after the war, assuming he survived. But even then, they hadn't really discussed what life with a traveling military man would be like for a Cajun girl.

No, he needed to take things slowly, cautiously.

"You think too much, Phillipe," she said, guessing at his dilemma.

Tugging her hand free, she danced ahead of him, deliberately wiggling her bottom at him.

And, yes, he could see by the outline of her trim pants that she had the heart-shaped ass he'd imagined while watching her at the USO last night. Praise God and pass the gumbo, as his mawmaw used to say when she'd looked out the window each morning to see if the sun was shining.

Yes, Louise's buttocks were a ray of sunshine to this soppy soldier. He laughed.

She laughed, too, and waited for him to catch up and

take her hand again. "Tomorrow's Sunday, and I'm free, but I have to be back to work on Monday," she told him.

"Can't you take a few days off?"

"I don't know. Yes, I do. I'll ask for the time off and make it up on the weekends. If my supervisor won't agree, I'll quit."

"I don't want you to lose your job, *chère*."

She shrugged. "There are always other jobs, but these days with you are more important."

His heart warmed at her words.

"This new S & R unit...the kind of work you'll be doing...is it dangerous?"

"No more than any other military action," he lied. "Actually, it's kind of ironic, but we'll probably be using the Higgins boats being made in your very factory."

"So, you'll be on boats," she said with relief.

"No, sweetheart. S & R frogmen will be sort of webfoot warriors. Advance men, in the water, up onto the beaches. Scanning the area for best landing sites for our troops. Searching out enemy gun locations. Then reporting back. That kind of thing."

"And you say that's not dangerous?" she scoffed.

"I didn't say it wasn't dangerous, just that it was no more than— Why are we talking about this stuff? I just want to talk about you, and me. I want to forget the war."

And they did. For three whole days, they spent practically every minute together until he dropped her off at her New Orleans cottage late at night and picked her up early each morning. They drove around, whenever he could scrounge up enough gas ration cards, swam, and sun bathed on Grand Terre Island, danced at the USO and a jazz nightclub, mostly necked while watching a movie, in fact necked whenever and wherever they got a chance, had dinner one night with his family, a raucous teasing good time with not just his parents but his younger brothers and sisters, and spent a few hours with Louise's parents at a shrimp festival in Houma.

The most amazing thing about Louise was the way she could make him laugh. She was always saying or doing something that caught him off guard.

Like the dream she related to him, in detail, in which they'd been Adam and Eve in the Garden of Eden.

"Really?" he'd inquired, sensing a trap. "And where exactly was this garden? Some paradise in Hawaii? Or the Holy Lands?"

"Actually, it wasn't a garden. It was a bayou. Right here in Loozeanna."

"Of course."

She'd slapped him on the arm for his sarcasm, but didn't even blink when he'd encouraged her to go on, "And were we naked?"

"Not quite. Instead of fig leaves, we wore cypress moss."

By then, he'd been grinning. "And the snake...?"

"It was a gator. And the apple was a sweet beignet."

He'd laughed, not sure if she was making it all up.

But she hadn't been done with him yet. "Doan'cha wanna know what we did that was so sinful, after we gorged ourselves on beignets?"

"No need, darlin'. I have dreams, too."

Or the time they passed a certain shop in the French Quarter that sold pin-up posters and pictures for randy soldiers to hang in their lockers or carry off to battle in their duffle bags. Some were merely racy, like the ones of Betty Grable in that famous white bathing suit and Rita Hayworth in a haymow, but others were downright pornographic, in a good way.

"I could do one of those," Louise had proclaimed.

"Louise!"

"Not the nude ones. The other ones. Like Rita Hayworth in the see-through nightie. Or that gal wearin' a sailor hat and shorts so short her cheeks are blushin'. Her other cheeks."

Phillipe had tried to steer her away from the shop window, embarrassed that others would overhear her. But she was not to be deterred.

"Mebbe I'll have one of these made and send it to you. A surprise present. I could be ridin' a gator, or reclinin' on a cypress log, jist ta give it local flavor. What do you think?"

Think? He'd been unable to think at the time, or speak, but he'd been smiling inside. He still was.

He'd drawn the line at the voodoo priestess who sold her wares from a seedy storefront on one of the side streets.

"Thass all right. I know more potions than Madame Fleurette does anyways. Do you wanna know what the best remedy is for the soldiers' complaint?"

No, he did not! And he'd told her so. With yet another laugh.

And now his leave was almost over, liberty cut short. Why was it that time moved so slowly when waiting for something good to happen, but moved faster than a duck in shark waters when the clock was ticking away toward some grief? And, yes, his departure was going to be a sort of grief to them both.

It was seven p.m. of his final night in Louisiana before heading out early tomorrow morning for Virginia. He'd already said his good-byes to his parents. His duffel bag was packed and ready for him to board the bus at the NSA base. Louise was waiting for him now to pick her up for "a special night" she had planned for him. Despite his coaxing, she'd refused to disclose details. Frankly, he didn't want any special activity, whether it be a fine restaurant meal, or dancing, or whatever; he just wanted to be with her, alone.

There was so much that hadn't been said yet, including those three magic words. And maybe they shouldn't be spoken aloud. Not now. Not when the timing was so half-ass crazy. Once spoken, a bond would be formed, a sort of promise for a future together, especially if the words were reciprocated. Who was he kidding? That bond was already there, blinking like a bloody neon sign.

Why did he always have to overthink everything? Why couldn't he be spontaneous like other guys? Jump into the water with both feet and worry about the perils later? After all, he was a really good swimmer. He was a sailor, after all.

Aaarrgh!

He was as confused about what to say or do as he had been three days ago.

How could he profess his love when there was every chance he might not come back? Wouldn't that hurt Louise more? Or was it better to take the chance?

Phillipe had never been much of a gambler.

Still...

And then there was the issue of his future, assuming he survived this blasted war. At least ten, maybe twelve years owed to the Navy, forced to move from base to base. Anywhere from San Diego to the Pacific. And military housing could be drab as hell. No, he just could not picture his Cajun girl anywhere but here near the bayou.

Besides, he knew how he'd been treated when he first moved up north, like an ignorant redneck Southern boy. It had been hard at first. Those Yankee girls would eat Louise alive.

Or would they? Sometimes he suspected Louise was stronger than she pretended to be...that old Southern belle image to keep up. But hadn't Southern women been proving since the Civil War that while they might be fragile flowers on the outside, they had stems of steel?

He'd just shaved and was staring at himself in the mirror above the sink in the officers' quarter bathroom at NSA, trying to put on a bright face. He was wearing his dress whites, at Louise's request. She'd told him that seeing him in uniform made her tummy tingle. What guy could refuse after that titillating image?

With disgust at his indecision over what to say on their final night together, he slapped on some Aqua Velva and made for his date.

One way or another, tonight was going to be a turning point. He hoped he made the right turn.

CHAPTER 4

You made me love you...

*L*ouise should have been nervous, but she was surprisingly calm as she led Phillipe into the lobby of Maison Rouge, a small, four-story hotel off the beaten path in the French Quarter.

She was tired of Phillipe's indecision. He hadn't even told her he loved her yet, *pour l'amour de Dieu*. She hadn't actually said the words herself, either, waiting for him to speak first. Enough! Time was running out. Sometimes a woman just needed to take matters into her own hands.

He looked so handsome in his uniform, and he must have shaved again this evening and gotten a haircut. When she looked at him, she felt kind of breathless...and tingly. Not just in her tummy, but all over. Other women looked at him, too, as they walked the short distance from his parked car to the hotel entrance. Louise was proud to be seen with him. Proud that he was hers. Or soon would be, if she had her way.

Louise had dressed special for the occasion, too, in a black, cap-sleeved, knee-length sheath with a sweetheart neckline and epaulette shoulder pads. Her last pair of pre-cious seamed nylons were held up by a new black lace gar-ter belt. In her dark hair, worn long tonight, tucked behind her ear on one side, she wore a waxy white gardenia. On her feet were her favorite red high heels. And, no, contrary to her mama's belief about red shoes, she was not pantyless...but almost, in scandalous sheer, see-through lace.

She knew she looked good, even without seeing the appreciative gleam in Phillipe's eyes as he continually gazed at her. The fool loved her, all right. His expressive eyes told her that, even if his lips hadn't...yet.

When they got inside, Phillipe said, "Ah, I knew your surprise was a good meal. Hopefully in a quiet corner, *chère*? And oysters! There's nothing like Gulf oysters, especially on my last night in town. Thank you, thank you." He started toward Chez Jacques, the restaurant that was located off the lobby, and was known for its specialty, Oysters Tabasco.

But Louise tugged on his hand and directed him the other way, toward the elevator. "Not so fast, sailor."

He arched his brows but said nothing while in the presence of the red-capped elevator operator.

"Third floor," she said.

Once they were out of the elevator, though, Phillipe

refused to move down the quiet hallway. "Louise, you can't be serious. We need to talk about this.

"Talk, talk, talk! That's all they'd done for the past three days. Not that she didn't like talking to Phillipe, but jeesh! Maybe he needed one of MawMaw's potions for when an old man's sap ran dry. "Juju tea mixed with a little goat weed will get the male juices runnin', lickety split," MawMaw used to tell her as they harvested the juju plant out in the swamps.

But that was a remedy Louise wasn't ready to try. "You don't wanna lay with me?" she asked, pretending to blink away tears, as she sidled over to Room 301.

"Lay? Lay? Holy mother of God! Of course I do. You know I do. But your reputation will be ruined."

She shrugged, inserting a key in the door and stepping inside. "Maybe. Maybe not. I reserved the room for my cousin, a famous Navy hero, who just got back from fighting over across the ocean. The poor boy needs a night of rest before going off ta his godmother's funeral in Lafayette."

Phillipe had no choice but to follow her inside. "This poor boy's godmother died ten years ago, and she lived in Baton Rouge."

She slammed the door behind him before he had a chance to skedaddle. "My belated sympathies."

"A Navy hero, huh? Seriously, *chère*, you should save your virginity for the man you marry."

Oh, those were fighting words. She glared at him and said, "If you're worried about how ta do this, I can help. I know...stuff." And she didn't mean how to mix any darn potion.

His face flushed. "I'm not a virgin."

She shrugged as if unsure whether to believe him. He couldn't have been prodded more if she'd thrown down a gauntlet.

"Well, hell's bells!" he said and tossed his hat up so that it circled in the air before landing smack dab on one post of the bed's footboard.

Impressive.

He unlaced his shoes and was toeing them off at the same time he was undoing the buttons on his jacket.

"What's your rush, sweetheart? Slow down. Look at all the preparations I made." She pointed to the wine bottle in an ice bucket and the plate of raw oysters swimming in Tabasco sauce, also on ice. "Aren't oysters supposed ta be an aphrodisiac?"

"Fuck your preparations and damn your aphrodisiac!" he said and didn't even apologize for his bad language.

Maybe she'd pushed him too hard.

Instead, he shrugged out of his jacket and shirt, placing them neatly on a nearby chair so they wouldn't get wrinkled. It was pure Phillipe, neat and careful, even under pressure. Well, his military training might have added to his fastidiousness, she conceded. He would get no demerits from her, although she couldn't have shaken him up too much if he still had the cool to maintain his obsession with order.

"I could always ask room service for an iron, and I

could press your uniform before you leave," she offered.

He growled. He actually growled at what she considered a very kind offer. "I have only nine hours, give or take, before I have to leave. I intend to make use of every minute. And none of it will involve an ironing board, unless you're stark naked, bent over it, posing for a pin-up."

Phillipe was no longer her "gentleman sailor," but a virile Louisiana man whose appetites had been suppressed for too long.

Heat flooded her face, then proceeded to unfurl down her body, causing the important parts to go all warm and melty like. Did he mean to make love to her for nine hours? Whoo-boy! She didn't know much about sex, and none of it from actual experience, but that seemed a might excessive. In a good way.

"And I don't hot damn well need instructions from a wet-behind-the-ears mudbug Cajun girl on how to do what comes naturally."

"Well, someone's got his tail feathers ruffled," she said.

He was beginning to unbuckle his belt when he glanced up at her. Then he did a little dance from foot to foot until he could step out of his pants, which he of course had to fold and lay over the chair. Only then did he smile, very slowly, and tell her, "It's not my tail feathers that are ruffled, *chère*. It's my tail." He waved a hand downward where he did, indeed, have a tail, or something way bigger than a feather, pointing outward. He was down to only a white undershirt, white undershorts, and white socks, and she couldn't help but notice his broad shoulders, narrow waist, and cute behind, not to mention the muscles defining his arms and legs. In fact, he looked good enough to be a male pin-up. Maybe they could have one of those pin-up pictures made, together. Wouldn't that be the bee's knees? She giggled.

"You're staring, Louise. Didn't your mama ever tell you it's not polite to stare?"

Mama never told her anything about this! She continued to stare, and the "feather" moved. "Lawdy, Lawdy, you do give a girl the vapors. I sure hope you have some of those thingamajigs in yer wallet. Guess I shoulda mentioned that before you undressed. Otherwise, you'll have ta run down to the drugstore, I s'pose."

His eyes went wide with surprise. "Do you mean prophylactics? Rubbers?"

She nodded, embarrassed.

"The military makes sure all its men know about... thingamajigs." In fact, he reached into the pocket of his pants and pulled out a small tin with Ramses imprinted on the lid. He placed it on the bedside table, then sank down to the side of the bed and said, "Your turn, Jezebel. You mentioned 'stuff' you know about. I'm all ears, and eyes."

Now that it came down to the nitty gritty, she wasn't sure she could do this. For courage, she flicked on the radio sitting on the dresser, and Glenn Miller's "In the Mood" came on. Certainly appropriate. "When I said that I knew stuff, I didn't mean that I know things from experience."

"Of course not," he said. Then, noticing her frown at his sarcasm, he added, "Did you read a book?"

"There are books about seducing a man?"

"Sed-seducing a man?" he sputtered out. "I thought by stuff, you meant the nuts and bolts of sex."

"There are nuts and bolts in sex? I didn't know that."

"Louise! If you say that you know stuff, then say you don't know this stuff from a book, or from practice, what exactly are you saying?"

"I know about flirting, of course. What Southern gal doesn't? The stuff I'm talkin' about is how ta make a man have sex with you when he resists."

His jaw dropped.

"Face it, sweetheart, you had every intention of goin' off ta war...or at least off ta Virginia, leavin' me intact."

He put his face in his hands and muttered something before raising his head. "And you plan on seducing me into changing my mind?"

"Uh-huh. But I wasn't exactly sure how to go about it, so I went ta my best friend Lettie Doucet and she sent me ta her cousin Violette. You know, Vi, don't you? She's 'bout yer age. Anyways, Vi hit some hard times after her husband was killed, and she works the night shift on Bourbon Street, if ya get my meanin'."

It took Phillipe several moments before he understood. "*Mon Dieu*! You went to a prostitute for seduction advice?"

She smiled. Now he understood. Would he be disgusted, or angry?

What he was, it turned out, was amused. He burst

out with laughter and fell back on the bed, laughing so hard tears rolled down his face and he held his sides as if in pain. Finally, he shimmied himself up onto the mattress so that his head was propped on the pillow and his legs were crossed at the ankles. With one hand, he motioned for her to proceed. "This ought to be good."

"It will be," she promised. "First off, a lady has to have good lingerie, according to Vi." She unzipped the back of her dress and let it slide down to puddle at her feet.

He gasped at first sight of her lacy nude bra and panties, not to mention the black garter belt, and sat up straighter.

"What do you think?" She arched her back so that her breasts stuck out, making them look bigger than they were.

"I think you're trying to torture me for not making the first move."

"Would I do that?" She fluttered her eyelashes at him. Then, with a quick turn, she looked back at him over her shoulder. "Are my seams straight?" When he just made a gurgling sound, she added, "Vi says that men like seamed stockings because the seams are like high-ways leading to paradise. Which is silly, of course. Like rear ends are anything but a place ta sit down on!"

Muttering something about heart-shaped gifts from the gods, he shot off the bed and was next to her before she could add her *coup de grace*, "I appear ta be all thumbs t'day. Would ya help me take off mah stockings?"

"I'll help you, all right," he muttered, picking her up

and carrying her over to the bed where he dumped her, then proceeded to crawl up and over her. Once he'd arranged himself over her, belly to belly, his thighs separating her legs, his arms braced over her head, he told her, "I'll take over from here, darlin'."

And he did.

~

In the mood...

"I LOVE YOU," he told her, before making love to her the first time. The words, finally spoken, put a seal on their relationship. It was not a sailor's line, polished over and over as a thigh opener, but a promise. A forever promise. That's why he had avoided the declaration for so long.

He guessed he was still more Cajun than he realized. When a Cajun man gave his heart, it was "till death do us part." Like his pawpaw said.

"Finally!" she said, nipping him on the jaw, then kissing it better.

Nip away, chère, he thought. There were parts of his body that appreciated her small gesture of pain/pleasure. In fact, there was one particular part that would welcome a nip-kiss. Maybe later. For now, he prodded, "Well?"

She pretended not to understand, at first, but then she sighed. "I love you, too, Phillipe, but I had to wait for you to say the words first."

"Why? You had no qualms about seducing me."

71

"That's different. There are some things that have to be done the old fashioned way."

So, she was Cajun at heart, too.

He was still lying atop her, braced on his extended arms to lessen his weight. Gazing down at her, he said, "I love you, Louise. Today, tomorrow, always. I can't make promises about our future, but I can't imagine it without you."

"I feel the same way, Phillipe." She put a hand to his cheek, lovingly. "Stop worryin' about me, how ta fit yer obligations with my inclinations. I'll be happy wherever you are."

It was a gentle loving then, because it was Louise's first time and because he wanted to express all the emotions he'd been holding back, for what reason he couldn't remember at the moment. First, he ordered her, "Don't move," as he jumped off the bed and shucked his skivvies and socks quicker than the blink of an eye. He was about to climb back onto the bed.

But Louise ordered, "No. Stand there a minute. Let me look at you first." She rose up on her elbows to get a better look.

He was a little embarrassed. Not by his nudity. He knew he had a good body, honed by military training. But it was probably the first time Louise had seen a man with a full-blown erection, and his was definitely full-blown.

"Oh, Phillipe, you are so beautiful."

He didn't know about beautiful, but he wasn't embarrassed anymore. "Your turn, darlin'," he said as he sat on the edge of the bed and proceeded to undress her, bit by bit. It was like unwrapping a much-anticipated Christmas gift.

First her bra, which revealed small but perfectly formed breasts with delicious pink tips. He touched them gently with his fingertips, causing her to arch upward and moan.

"You like that?" he asked.

"Heavenly," she replied.

When he leaned down and took one into his mouth, licking the nipple with his raspy tongue, she moaned, "More."

He smiled and moved downward. Undoing her garters, then rolling the nylons down her legs. She still had on her red heels which he had to remove first. He had plans for those high heels, later. The famous Betty Grable back view, glance back over the shoulder, white bathing suit with high heels pin-up, came to mind. Not that he'd ever examined the photo more than, oh, say, a hundred times. Except Louise would be sans bathing suit, in his imagined pin-up. Just the sexy-hot, red heels. And maybe her hair would be down and not upswept. And, of course, her hair was dark, not Betty Grable blond. And maybe she would have this same flower in her hair. So many possibilities!

And, holy Cajun catfish, but this present scenario was much more exciting than any sailor's locker pin-up could ever be.

Louise was left with only the wispy, see-through panties now. True to her outrageous form, Louise bent one knee, lifted her arms above her head, and posed for him. With her dark hair spread on the pillow, with the flower still behind one ear, she would win any competition for best pin-up model, ever. Forget Betty Grable—Louise was hot, hot, hot. Not that he would ever want to share this picture with any other guy.

With the scant garment removed and tossed back over his shoulder, he began a slow loving. Kisses...many, many kisses. And caresses. Tentative fingers exploring all her secret places. And words, husky words of appreciation for all her tempting parts.

And Louise, innocent as she was of the actual sexual act, was a quick learner. In fact, she soon taught him a few things about arousal and the rise of excitement to a fever pitch. Were these tricks she'd been taught by Vi, the prostitute, or was she a born seductress?

In any case, the gentle loving was a slow torture for them both, until Louise grabbed hold of him right where a man didn't want to be grabbed, and demanded, "Now! I've waited long enough."

He saw stars for a moment. But then, who was he to argue, especially with his cock in a vise?

It was over way too soon. Louise claimed it hadn't hurt, much, and he kept telling her how much he loved her, and she repeated the words back at him. Now that the words had been spoken, they couldn't seem to say them enough.

She spent a good half hour exploring his body. She was fascinated by the dark hairs on his chest and the trail it made down, down, down his belly. She played with his male nipples and stuck the tip of her tongue in his belly button. She even examined his balls which she thought were funny. He would have been offended by that if he wasn't so appreciative of the fondling. And, of course, the witch loved the effect her efforts were having on his favorite part, which she named *Le Buche*, the log.

When she tried to climb on top of him...another idea from the great Violette?...he told her, "It's too soon. You must be sore."

"Hah!" she said and took matters into her own hands. Literally. This second time, she learned about female orgasms, and she couldn't stop talking about it:

"Phillipe! That was better than necking and kissing, combined. Better than sweet beignets with café au lait on a Sunday morning in Nawleans.

"Do all women know about this?

"It felt like little explosions goin' off in my body. Glory be!"

Mon Dieu! This has to be the best kept secret, ever.

"Is it like this all the time, Phillipe? Is it? Oh, I surely hope so."

Does it feel the same way for a man? Oh, only one at a time per bout. That doesn't seem fair."

But is there a limit on how many bouts there can be in one night?"

Wait till I tell my mother she left the best part out when she gave me that sex talk."

"Um, I don't think discussing this with your mother is a good idea," he suggested.

"Maybe not," she agreed and grinned at him.

"I think I may have awakened the tiger here,"

Phillipe said, laughing at her enthusiasm, and kissing the top of her head as he drew her tight against his side with her face on his chest.

"You implyin' that I'm a tiger, *cher*? Well, just wait till you hear me roar," she said and nipped his chin, at the same time inching one knee up and over his thigh."

I'd rather hear you purr, darlin'."

And she did. A lot.

After that, they ate oysters and drank wine in bed and talked about everything but the future. That horse had already left the barn, and they weren't going to dwell on it anymore. At least not during these precious hours they had left together.

By morning, the love they'd professed for the first time the evening before was now firmly cemented by fierce and intense lovemaking, and sweet words of promise and hope.

"No, don't get up," he said when he was fully dressed and ready to leave by four a.m.

"But I was going to come see you off on the bus."

He shook his head. "I want to remember you this way."

And so Phillipe was alone when he boarded the bus that would take him to Little Creek, Virginia, and the beginning of a new adventure as an amphibian scout. But he was smiling as he left his homeland.

He would return, guar-an-teed.

CHAPTER 5

As time goes by...

O ver the next year or so, Louise grew to love Phillipe more and more, even though they were apart for most of that time.

He was kind. He showed that not just in his consideration of her feelings for the bayou, but how he treated his military buddies, spending his off hours teaching some of them the academic skills needed to pass written tests, and his own family, who were in the same financial straits as her own.

He was loving. The letters he wrote often included newspaper or magazine clippings about couples who overcame insurmountable odds to be together. Who knew he had such a romantic side!

He was sexy. Oh, my! And not just in bed.

He was even developing a sense of humor. The photograph he sent of himself, wearing bathing trunks, a diving mask, and flippers, standing in a desert some-where, was priceless.

And the body he was developing with his military exercises, not to mention all that swimming....well, all she could say was, "Ooh la la!"

They exchanged dozens of letters, many of his on the required V-mail microfilm paper when he was out of the country on some mission or other, with lines blocked out that might disclose his location or military activity. "Loose lips sink ships," was the motto of the day. As if she would know Tunisia or Palermo from Timbuktu! Although she did buy a pocket atlas from the used book-store on Canal Street.

It was those times, though, when she didn't receive a letter or a rare phone call, weeks at a stretch, that scared her most. She knew by his "silences" that he must be on a mission, somewhere dangerous, where he might be wounded, or never return.

The relief when she heard from him again was beyond description. Usually, she had to go off some-where by herself afterward to cry her eyes out. But that was nothing compared to those women, and she knew a few, who got the hated "regret to inform" telegrams telling them of a loved one's demise. The poor over-worked telegram boys who delivered those messages had come to be called "Angels of Death."

She kept every single letter of Phillipe's in a Whit-man's Sampler tin she'd been given for Christmas when she was twelve years old, the Salmagundi mosaic one featuring the pretty blond woman in profile. Some of the fine paper of his letters were frayed and worn from her constant rereading. A few were tear-stained and blurry. To her alarm, the box was almost full. When she'd first started saving Phillipe's letters from the military base in Virginia, she'd thought the war would soon be over and the box too big. Now, she could barely close the lid.

And, in fact, Phillipe was no longer with the S & R teams, but had instead moved over to some unit involving underwater demolition whose base was in Fort Pierce, Florida. He'd explained that there were now five different groups operating as amphibian special forces units: the Scouts and Raiders (S & R), Naval Combat Demolition Unit (NCDUs), Underwater Demolition Teams (UDTs), the Office of Strategic Services (OSS), and Motor Torpedo Boat Squadrons. Why he'd chosen to move from scouting and raiding, which was dangerous enough, to something involving explosives was beyond her.

When Louise had relayed all this information to her mother, Mama agreed with her dismay and made *tsking* sounds of commiseration. "Boys allus like things that go boom."

Her papa, who had no less than twelve hunting rifles...TWELVE!...and who scared away half the birds in the bayou when he plinked tin cans off the garden fence, and who'd once tried to dynamite a stump in their back yard but, instead, blew away half of her mother's vegetable patch, sighed and said, "Phillipe is one lucky somabitch, 'scuse mah French. I'd like ta blow up one them Nazi U-boats mahself."

Suffice it to say, Louise prayed a lot during those days, especially when she read newspaper accounts referring to the "elite combat divers," or "frogmen" and she just knew Phillipe was involved, somehow. For example, there was Operation Torch, the Allied invasion of North Africa in which some of these brave swimmers had cut the enemy's underwater cables so that American ships could move safely into those waters and insert their soldiers. All of the men in Phillipe's unit had received some kind of medals for their work there.

Louise didn't know much about military commendations, but when she'd told her father about Phillipe's particular medal, something involving a Navy cross, his eyes had gone wide with a mixture of admiration and horror. Before he'd had a chance to bite his tongue, he said, "I thought they only gave those things to dead sailors."

Then, too, there were horrendous newspaper accounts of Operation Husky, the Allied invasion of Sicily, that relied heavily on these special forces to make way for the ground troops. Among the fatalities in Sicily had been Chief Petty Officer Franklin Mitchell from Boston, a close friend of Phillipe's. Mitch had considered it hilarious that she was "Louise from Louisiana." When she tried to talk about Mitch, Phillipe's face closed over, and he refused to discuss the circumstances of his death. In fact, Louise wasn't even sure if Phillipe had participated in that mission.

Not to mention the increasing news coming out of Germany of atrocities being meted out to the Jewish people. Hard to believe that so many were being killed or kept in filthy camps just because of their religion. Jimmy John Doucet, a distant cousin who'd gotten a medical discharge from the Army after some battle in France, said he'd met a Jewish rabbi who'd escaped from one of those work camps, and he looked like a walking skeleton.

And there was no dodging the horrors of war even when going to an occasional movie. The news reels shown before the films depicted such gruesome fatalities of the various battles that a person could scarcely sit and laugh afterward at Charlie Chaplin or Abbott and Costello.

She and Phillipe saw each other on occasional visits when he came back to Louisiana on short liberties, but as the war wore on, Phillipe's face was more and more stiff, and his eyes deadened. The same was true of many military men she saw at the USO, where she still volunteered. Leastways, that's how Phillipe always looked when he first came home. By the end of a liberty, he was more his old self again. Until the next time.

Louise had made one bus trip up to Virginia early on, which she'd hated. Not the bus itself, or being with Phillipe, which was of course wonderful, but the strange territory where there was a vast ocean but no bayous, where everyone seemed in a hurry all the time, where people spoke differently and looked at her strangely when she asked for a beignet or gumbo on a restaurant menu. She was the proverbial fish out of water outside Louisiana, and this wasn't even *north* north, she was told repeatedly. Always, she tried to be positive with Phillipe.

And besides, he was stationed in Florida now, which was almost as warm as Louisiana. They even had bayous there, she was told.

So, Louise had started to avoid both newspapers and movie theaters. Instead, she spent more time at her parents' home on Bayou Black where they had their own kinds of problems.

First off, her father had suffered a stroke, which left him partially paralyzed, unable to continue working on the shrimp boats, and requiring her mother's constant home care. Even before that, he'd been bent over with a shrimper's hump, old before his time, from years of back-breaking work. When shrimping, the catch was dumped onto the foredeck, and the men had to either bend over or squat to "pick" the shrimp, which meant rooting out the by-catch, like squid, or baby crabs, or junk fish. Not to mention the strain of hauling up heavy nets or lifting hundred-pound bait boxes.

Louise would have moved back home to help, but her salary as a typist was needed more than ever to help her parents get by. Cajuns were proud people, and signing up for public relief was abhorrent to them. Instead, Louise took on more overtime work at Higgins. Besides, she needed something to keep her busy while Phillipe was away.

Then another crisis occurred. Louise's brother Frank, an Army corporal serving in the Pacific, was declared missing in action, possibly a prisoner of war.

In the meantime, this Sunday afternoon in September, Louise and her mother were out in the swamps gathering herbs for her mother's folk healing business.

"How is yer *traiteur* business doin', Mama? I mean, people are so poor these days with the war and all. They don't hardly have money fer anything."

"I'm doin' fine, 'specially with yer help, sweet one. My customers doan allus have money, but they pay me somehow. Eggs, milk, and wild mushrooms. Apples, peaches, plums, and cherries, by the bushel, which I can allus use or cook up inta preserves. If we had more traffic out thisaway, I could set up a produce stand out front."

Every time Louise returned to the city, she carried with her a poke full of jellies or canned applesauce, some of which she donated to the USO.

"And fish...Lawdy, I get so much fish I gotta smoke 'em fer later eatin'. I doan even miss all the shrimps yer daddy usta bring home. Once in a while, I get a turtle which makes a fine soup." Her mother laughed. "I doan suppose you and yer friends would want a possum or two. I've eaten so much possum stew I'm about ta gag."

"Thanks, but no thanks, Mama," she declined graciously as she continued to row. Actually, possum wasn't so bad when cooked properly. "We don't have time fer much cookin' after work."

"Or the rations to buy readymade food all the time," her mother guessed.

She was right there. They were always running out of ration stamps for food, gas, coal, nylons, practically everything. Even so, single women didn't want to spend hours stewing game of any kind when they could be out hunting their own game of another kind. Men.

"So, any particular plants we're lookin' for t'day?" Louise asked. They were already deep in the bayou, a half mile from home.

Her mother nodded. "Somethin' what'll aid in yer father's paralysis and speakin' problems. Snake Tears is an old remedy fer stroke that MawMaw tol' me about. The plant is hard ta find, but I checked her ol' book, and there was a drawin'. The leaves look lak the buttons on a rattlesnake's tail, but tear-shaped."

MawMaw Doucet, her mother's grandmother, had kept a clothbound book of "receipts" with pencil drawings of swamp plants for every ailment under the bayou sun. The book had been added to by every generation of women with the "gift" since then—everything from "Women's Complaint" to "Man Trouble." Louise knew now that they referred to menstrual pains and male impotence, but when she'd been a child and asked what they meant, her mother had said, "Men are women's biggest complaint, and women are men's biggest trouble."

The "receipts" included remedies for all the usual illnesses: fever, rheumatiz, headaches, Arthur-itis, swollen glands, rashes, the fits, and open wounds, with a special section for "gator bites." Her favorite had been dried dog dung mixed with honey for sore throats. Her papa had called that one "Sweet Shit," which always prompted a swat with a dishtowel from her mama. Of course, that was before he lost his voice.

"Shouldn't you be followin' the doctor's orders fer Daddy?" Louise asked.

"I am, but sometimes the old remedies work better."

Louise couldn't argue with that, though she couldn't imagine ever prescribing "Sweet Shit" to anyone. A sure case of the cure being worse than the ailment.

Her mother was wearing an old pair of fishermen's hip boots hiked up with suspenders to her chest, and a long-sleeved shirt that must have been Frank's during his teenage years. Louise wore waders, too, but hers were thigh-high over her slacks, which were tucked into the boots. She wore a long-sleeved shirt, too, one of Daddy's old Long John uppers that had been washed to paper thinness.

It was so blistering hot today that she would have much preferred a bathing suit, but the mosquitoes and no-see-ums would eat her alive. As it was, she and her mother had slathered themselves with a homemade bug-repellant salve, and they wore lavender herb ribbons around their necks.

The boots were a necessity because some of the grounds they traipsed through looked and felt more like chocolate pudding than packed bayou dirt. Besides, you never knew when a snake might strike, without warning. The perils of swamp living!

"So, where do we find this Snake Tears plant?"

"Yer great-grandmother drew a map to a small island where it used to flourish, but you know what the bayou streams and islands are like. Here t'day, gone t'morrow."

"Phillipe has a pilot friend who told him that the

Loo-zee-anna bayous from up above look like a crocheted doily. All those twists and turns."

"And every time there's a big storm, the bayous disappear or go in a different direction," her mother added. "Even so, I think I kin follow the general direction of MawMaw's map. I did find it once a few years back when Cousin Joe had his stroke. You remember him, they called him Smokey 'cause he allus had a cigarette danglin' from his mouth."

"Did Snake Tears help him?"

"Not a bit. He had too much smoke in his system fer anythin' ta work, at that point. When he passed, the doctor cut him open and said his lungs were black as coal."

They found the Snake Tears plant, along with some other roots and leaves that her mother would store in her herbal pantry. Some of them were edible, like the cattails whose various versatile parts could be used to make poultices, or as a downy buffer for a baby's bottom to prevent chafing, or added to salads for a yummy crunch.

"Y'know, Mama, I'm far from an expert on folk medicine, but it amazes me how much I've gleaned just by being around you and MawMaw."

Her mother shrugged and said, "*Mais oui*! You have the gift."

Louise smiled. "Lot of good that gift will do me if I'm livin' in some far-off land with Phillipe."

"Whass this? Am I the las' one ta know that yer engaged?" She glanced at Louise's ringless left hand and arched her brows.

"No, no! Nothing official. Phillipe is afraid to make any promises for fear of jinxing us. The war and everything."

Her mother nodded. "Jist like some couples expecting a baby don't wanna set up a nursery too soon, jist in case somethin' happens."

"If he doesn't ask me soon, I'll probably ask him."

"Louise!"

"What difference does it make? We're in love, and we're going to be together after the war."

"And it won't be here on the bayou when you're ...together?"

"It can't be. Not at first. Phillipe has years of military obligations, even after he finishes his medical schooling."

"Where will that be?"

"I don't know. Possibly Virginia to finish his schooling. Then, wherever the Navy sends him as a military doctor. All the Navy bases have married housing."

"What will you do when he's in school, or off bein' a sailor doctor?"

"Work."

"As what?"

"Anything. Typist, like I am now. Or something else. I could even train to be a nurse."

"But not a *traiteur*?"

Louise shook her head slowly. "Maybe someday, if... when...we return to the bayou."

"I'll be long gone by then." Her mother sighed.

"You will not! You're young yet. Only fifty. You have lots of years left, Mama."

"Mebbe so, mebbe not." Her mother sighed again. "I had dreams of you workin' by my side and eventually takin' over."

"That could still happen," Louise said, but even she didn't see the likelihood of that happening, not anytime in the near future, not with Phillipe's commitments to the Navy.

"When do you expect to see Phillipe again?"

"Probably not till Christmas."

"He'll have a leave then?"

Louise nodded. "His team has been promised a one-week liberty at the end of December." She couldn't speak for a moment over the lump in her throat, but then she revealed, "After that, they're heading overseas fer further training."

They both understood what that meant. The newspapers and radio had been predicting for weeks that something big was going to happen in Europe to put an end to this bloody war. Bloody being the key word.

Her mother squeezed her hand and said, "Well, then, you'll have to make this the best possible Christmas ever for Phillipe."

She would. And she already knew what she was going to give Phillipe for a Christmas gift.

CHAPTER 6

I'll be home for Christmas (if good ol' Bing, and Uncle Sam, have their way)...

*P*hillipe Prudhomme, sporting new second-lieutenant stripes on his dress blue travel uniform, stood in the terminal of the Fort Pierce airfield with a bunch of his buddies, waiting to hitch rides on various troop supply planes heading in various directions. He would be going to Fort Polk, then on to Bayou Black, in Louisiana for a much-anticipated ten-day liberty. Others, carrying topcoats and pea jackets, were heading north to New England and beyond.

Piped-in music played traditional Christmas songs... Bing Crosby, Rosemary Clooney, Perry Como, Dinah Shore, and the like. And a half-assed attempt had been made to decorate the gloomy corrugated steel building with fake holly and poinsettias. A palm tree outside blinked with strings of multi-colored lights in the pre-dawn blackness.

The mood was forced cheerfulness because each and every one of his NCDU teammates knew with a certainty that this would be their last chance to connect with family before leaving for Europe and what was rumored to be the big bang ending of the war. Some of them would not be returning.

Phillipe had started out with S & Rs in Little Creek, Virginia almost a year and a half ago where they'd trained till they dropped and then trained some more in a crash course to become proficient in demolitions, commando tactics, cable-cutting, and rubber boat maneu-vers. Only a few months later, they'd participated in Operation Torch in North Africa, where they'd succeeded in cutting cable and net barriers across the Wadi Sebou River, allowing the USS Dallas to traverse the river and insert U.S. Rangers who captured the airdome. Every one of his teammates, himself included, received a Navy Cross for their efforts in that hair-raising venture.

Then, only a few months after that, the S & R unit moved to Fort Pierce where Phillipe was asked to move over to the NCDU unit, where he and his fellow webfoot warriors prepared and continued to prepare for Opera-tion Overlord, the amphibious landings for D-Day in France, which would occur sometime during the upcoming year. In fact, he and thirty-three of his NCDUs would be reporting to London after this liberty for final training and instructions.

Maybe then, this damn war would end.

And he could get back to living.

And Louise.

He smiled to himself, knowing that in just a few hours, he would be holding his sweet Cajun girl again. Would she like the surprise he was bringing for her?

"Oh, crap! The loo-ie is grinning again," one of the swabbies in his unit remarked. Seaman Jason Saunders, at eighteen, was the comedian of the teams, but serious as all get out when it came to the Navy, having come from a long line of sailors, many of them lifers who started out at the bottom of the enlisted pole, just like Jason had.

"Y'all got it wrong. He's jist happy 'cause he's been a good boy this year, and Santa's gonna fill his stocking with Christmas goodies. Pralines and Mardi Gras beads and a crawfish beer bottle opener, fer example." This from Petty Officer Mike Landry, a fellow Southerner, from Baton Rouge.

Another Petty Officer, Frank Phillips, the oldest of the group at thirty-two, piped in, "Hah! The only goodies I'm interested in are wrapped in a garter belt and see-through brassiere."

"After the Hell Week the shavetail put us through last week, Santa might give him a lump of coal, instead," Saunders said, grinning to show his teasing was just in fun.

Ever since he'd gotten his promotion last week, Phillipe's men had been teasing him. Their remarks were inappropriate and certainly against military protocol, but he wasn't about to pull rank on them now, not in this situation, and not as they were just about to go on liberty.

Still, he had to speak up on one point. "Hey, Hell Week wasn't my idea. Commander Kauffman was responsible for that exercise in torture. And look at it this way...we're all a lot more buff for enduring it."

"And bruised," Saunders pointed out.

"Who ever heard of running five miles before breakfast?" Phillips complained. "I've been in the Navy for seven years, and the only running we ever did, after boot camp, was to the chow hall."

"I usta love swimming, but not so much anymore," Landry put in. "I think I swallowed more salt water last week than my entire life."

"It was the drownproofing exercise that did it for me. Whoo-boy! I thought I was a goner, for sure."

Phillipe let them go on and on. He knew they were in the NCDU unit by choice, and were proud to be called webfoot warriors. Besides, Phillipe was on liberty time now, and he was determined to enjoy every minute of it.

On the plane, his seatmate was a white-knuckled young Marine from Lafayette. He was clutching the armrests like they were ballasts in a bayou wind storm.

"Fear of flying?" Phillipe asked.

"Nah. Fear of wedlock, with the emphasis on *lock*," he replied. At Phillipe's arched brows, he explained, "My girl, Jillie, has a bun in the oven, and her daddy has a shotgun that he plans to aim at my private parts."

"And you don't want to get married?"

"Oh, Jillie and me were gonna get hitched, eventually. Jist not this soon."

Phillipe nodded his understanding. In some ways, he envied the young fellow, having the decision taken out of his hands. Which was ridiculous, of course. He had good reasons for wanting to wait until after the war to start a future with Louise.

When they landed at Fort Polk, the first person he saw when he emerged onto the plane steps was Louise standing in the terminal doorway. How could he miss her! She was wearing a red velvet dress, tight on top and swirly on the bottom, edged with white fur on the neckline, cuffs, and hem. Black high-heeled boots and a Santa cap on her head completed the picture. *And did I mention red lipstick?*

Every man's Christmas fantasy!

He smiled as he stepped onto the tarmac. Dropping his duffel bag onto the ground, he opened his arms and she came running into his embrace. He lifted her off the ground and buried his face in her neck. She smelled of her Tabu perfume and Louise skin, a deadly combination to a war-weary soldier.

"I've missed you so much, *chère*," he said.

"Not half as much as me, my love," she countered. There were tears in her dark Cajun eyes.

She reached up and kissed him then, and it was no sweet welcome brush of lips. It was desperate and hungry, expressing all the pent-up emotions they were both feeling.

A male voice passing by, probably Landry, Phillipe

figured by the Southern drawl, hooted out, "Lookee, lookee, the looie and his Lou-ise."

Phillipe couldn't care less. He would probably be covered with Louise's lipstick. He couldn't care less about that, either.

A short time later, they were in his car in the parking lot. She'd picked it up from his parents' place where it had been stored in a shed. Along the way, they'd stopped repeatedly to kiss, or just look at each other.

"I have a present for you," she told him when they came up for a breather. They were still sitting in the parking lot.

"Uh-uh. No opening presents before Christmas," he told her.

"It's not that kind of present."

He waggled his eyebrows at her.

She laughed. "It's not that kind of present, either."

"Okay, sweetheart. Give."

"My roommates have all gone home for Christmas, and they won't be back until New Year's Day."

It took Phillipe only a second to figure out, today was Wednesday, Christmas was on Saturday, and New Year's Day was the following Saturday. That meant ten whole days alone.

He made it to Louise's cottage in New Orleans in record time, barely noticing the holly and glittering lights that adorned the faded yellow house with green shutters. He did pause for a second and laugh when he saw the little Christmas tree in the front room decorated with nothing but lights and little sea shells. He knew, without asking, that the shells were the ones she'd collected on the Grand Terre Island beach they'd visited one time.

A short time later, a way too short time later, they were naked in her bed, and sated. Well, relatively sated. He lay on his back and she was on her side with her face on his chest and one leg over his thigh.

"Well, that was embarrassing," he said, kissing the top of her head.

"What? Me? Did I do something wrong?"

"No, not you, darlin'. Me. No soldier wants to be that quick on the trigger."

"Oh," she said, understanding. Then she looked up at him and grinned. "Maybe I better check the barrel to make sure there's no malfunction."

She did. Thoroughly. And this time, the lovemaking was a little slower and more satisfying, for both of them.

"Where'd you learn how to do that?" he asked, afterward.

"From a book."

"What book? Don't tell me your prostitute friend is giving you books now."

"No, Vi didn't give me any books, and you shouldn't call her a prostitute just because she was on hard times. She's remarried now, anyhow, and lives on a farm up north with her Air Force husband's family."

"Okaaay," he said slowly. Louise tended to go off on a tangent at the least question. "So, where did you get these books?"

"My roommate, Cheryl Ann, has a brother-in-law whose cousin has a collection."

"What precisely are we talking about here?"

"*The Adventures of Tom Jones. Moll Flanders*. The *Kama Sutra*. Lordy, Lordy, you should see those pictures! Lots of men's magazines. Then, of course, I got an early copy of that new book, *Forever Amber*. I had no idea…"

And off she went on another tangent. He barely listened, just watched her animated features. Lord, he loved this woman! So much! Was he really here with her where he'd dreamed of being all these months?

"Are you hungry?" she inquired finally, when she took a break.

"Starved. I haven't had a bite since I ate a stale Christmas cookie in the Fort Pierce air terminal this morning."

"Oh, my poor baby! Well, I've got homemade beignets that I made last night with the last of my sugar ration," she began, off and running on another tangent. "Mama's teaching me how to make them, just like the Café du Monde. No coffee, though. That's impossible to find these days. But I do have sweet tea in the ice box. I also bought you one of your favorite muffalettas from Central Grocery. And, speaking of Mama, she sent some shrimp gumbo for your homecoming, and half of a Figgy Buttermilk Cake, which is a compliment to you since she hasn't made that since Daddy died."

"How's she doing?"

"All right. She keeps busy with her *traiteur* work."

"I'm sorry I couldn't come for your daddy's funeral. At the time, I was…um, away. I'm not sure I could have got a liberty anyhow."

"Mama understood, and as I told you before, she appreciated the Mass card you sent. So, what'll it be? Beignets, gumbo, muffaletta, or cake?"

"All of those," he said.

She rose from the bed and proceeded to walk toward the doorway when she paused and gave her bottom a little wiggle just to show that she knew he was watching her nude display. The minx!

After going into the bathroom to relieve his bladder and dispose of the used rubbers, he pulled on a pair of undershorts and went out to the little kitchen, which was only big enough to hold a stove, ice box, Hoosier style cabinet, and a chrome table with a Formica top, flanked by two vinyl-covered chairs.

Louise had donned his undershirt, which reached all the way to her knees. "Ta da!" she said, waving a hand to display the feast she'd laid out on the table.

He ate voraciously. Two helpings of everything, even the beignets which were a bit limp. Not that he would tell Louise.

"We should probably go out to visit my family this evening," he said. "I have a few gas ration stamps."

"And I have some I saved up," she told him as she began to clear the table. "Do you want to take a bath first?"

"Only if you're in the tub with me."

She put a forefinger to her chin as if pondering his question. "First, I have a question for you. It's about those books I mentioned."

"Uh-huh," he said dubiously, seeing the mischievous glint in her eyes.

"Well, there was one thing I didn't understand. It was in one of those men's magazines."

"Go on," he prodded, not unaware of the rosy hue that now adorned her cheeks. This ought to be good if it could make his wild Cajun girl blush.

"What is sixty-nine?"

They never made it to the tub until much later.

CHAPTER 7

***There was a whole lot of ho-ho-ho-ing
going on...***

*L*ouise accompanied Phillipe when he visited
with his family that night, and they brought
Louise's mother with them. Her mother didn't
complain a lot, but Louise knew she was lonely and
worried about Frank. There was still no word on her
brother. Phillipe was wearing his dark blue dress
uniform, which he usually didn't like to do while on
liberty, but he explained that his family liked to see him
in military attire.

Phillipe's family house was a joyful place, especially
at Christmastime. The stilted house, made of logs, had a
wide back porch that fronted Bayou Black, about thirty
feet away. Every window had a candle in it, and garlands

and wreaths of pine boughs and Spanish moss hung with red bows in swags here and there.

In the yard was a chicken coop, which was something new. She shouldn't be surprised. Lots of families were raising their own table fare in these times of tight rationing.

"Merry Christmas! Ho, ho, ho! Welcome, welcome," Phillipe's father, Zachary Prudhomme, said cheerily from the open doorway, but he only had eyes for his son, whom he hadn't seen for months. Louise heard him whisper, "We are so proud of you, son." His mother Nadine greeted them the same way, and her hug of her oldest son was even tighter than his father's.

They greeted Louise, as well, with kisses to the cheek, and then hugged her mother, too.

"Alma, bless yer heart, ya brought yer famous Figgy Buttermilk Cake, dint you?" Nadine said to Louise's mother on seeing the cake tin she carried. "Ya shouldn't have, but, Lordy, I cain't wait to slice me a piece."

Louise and Phillipe had brought a ham which they'd purchased with their combined rations.

"Louise, yer lookin' mighty pretty t'night," Zachary said. She was wearing the Santa outfit again, at Phillipe's urging. "No wonder mah son is so smitten. If I was twenty years younger, I might give him a run fer his money."

"More like thirty years, you old goat," Phillipe's mother said with a smile.

"Smitten? Do I look smitten?" Phillipe asked Louise in an undertone.

"Totally," she replied.

Once inside the large room which was a reverse L-shape, the bottom leg being the kitchen which opened onto a large living room, she saw it was filled to over-flowing with family. There was Phillipe's pawpaw, who remained seated with one leg propped on a hassock; he was suffering from gout, Phillipe had told them on the way over. His pawpaw had tears in his eyes when Phillipe leaned over him to give him a hug.

Also there was Phillipe's sister Josette, who was there with her husband Mark Bastian and their toddler, Michael. Phillipe's brother Samuel, who was twelve years younger at fourteen, was playing with a large, mixed-breed collie on the floor. His sister Mary Mae, or MaeMae, at sixteen, sat on the couch with her boyfriend Rufus LeBlanc. The only one missing was Phillipe's sister Felice, who was twenty-one and serving as a WAC nurse somewhere overseas on a hospital ship.

Christmas music was playing on the phonograph, and the smell of pine needles from the brightly lit tree in the corner and spicy food cooking in the kitchen, plus the constant chatter and laughter contributed to the overall warm atmosphere. Family. That was important, Louise realized, and it was sad that her mother lived alone. Louise vowed then and there that she and Phillipe would have at least four children someday, maybe even five, and she told Phillipe so in a whisper as they sat on the floor, holding hands, next to the tree.

"Whatever you say, darlin'. I'm feelin' like Santa Bountiful tonight. Ho, ho, ho!" Phillipe said and kissed their joined hands, a gesture which didn't go unnoticed by some in the room.

Phillipe's pawpaw called out, "Remember what I tol' you, Phillipe, 'bout the Prudhomme Whammy?"

"I remember," Phillipe said with a wink at his grandfather.

Phillipe's father, overhearing, looked at PawPaw, then Phillipe, then back at PawPaw, and remarked, "Talk about!"

"What's a Prudhomme Whammy?" she asked Phillipe.

"I'll tell you later."

After another hour of food, conversation, even singing, they took Louise's mother home with promises to pick her up the next night for Midnight Mass at Our Lady of the Bayou Church. She and Phillipe were probably fooling no one with their little white lies about him needing to stay at the NAS officer quarters and her staying in the New Orleans cottage because of her work at the Higgins plant. But no one said anything.

They spent the next two days and nights making love, shopping for Christmas presents, making love, wrapping Christmas presents, making love, visiting the USO where they danced three sets, then went home to make love again. Phillipe was teaching her some things that weren't mentioned in the books. He claimed he'd learned it all in Anatomy 101, a college pre-med course in which he'd excelled with a final A-plus grade. She would give him an A-plus, too.

Once he'd pretended he was Santa...a nude Santa...

bringing her a special present. He had her Santa hat on his head and a red bow tied on his you-know-what. "Ho, ho, ho!" he said.

Before they left the cottage on Christmas Eve, Phillipe turned serious. "Let's exchange our gifts now," he suggested. "We'll be too tired when we get back, and I'd like to sleep in tomorrow morning." He waggled his eyebrows at that last statement.

"Okay. Let me go get mine." When she returned to the small living room with a large, gaily wrapped package in the form of a cylinder, she saw Phillipe was down on one knee.

She gasped and set his gift on the sofa. "Phillipe?"

He held out a little velvet box with a diamond ring inside. "Will you marry me, Louise? After this war is over, will you be my bride? I can't promise where we'll live or what I'll be doing, but I promise this: I will love you forever." His voice was husky with emotion as he spoke.

Tears misted her eyes as she said, "Yes. Yes, yes, yes!"

He stood and slipped the ring on her finger. "I know it's small," he started to say.

"It's perfect," she countered, and they kissed to seal the engagement. Then they kissed again.

"What made you change your mind?" she asked. "You've been adamant about waiting till after the war is over."

"We'll still wait to get married, but I love you, and you love me, and it seemed foolish not to put a ring on your finger."

She smiled, admiring her ring on an extended arm. But then, she said, "I forgot. Your gift."

"What are you up to, darlin'?" he asked, noticing the grin she couldn't hide.

"Me?" she said with mock innocence, handing him the present.

Inside the cardboard mailing tube were two posters. Pin-up posters, actually. In one, she was wearing a sailor suit, fitted to her feminine form with an exaggerated cleavage which she did not have. In the other she was wearing a red silk robe. The artist had wanted her to wear a black, see-through negligee, but that was a bit too racy, even for her.

Phillipe examined them both, in detail, then looked up at her. "You minx!"

"Do you like them?"

"I love them."

"I didn't frame them because I thought they would be too difficult to carry with you. And I had smaller size copies made, which will fit in your wallet."

"You couldn't have given me a better gift," he said.

"Likewise," she replied.

"I'll have to hide them from the guys. I wouldn't want them drooling over my girl."

"I don't care if anyone else sees them. Nothing naughty is showing."

"Do we have time for me to thank you...better?"

"We have to leave in a half hour."

"That'll do."

They were almost late for Midnight Mass.

Making Christmas memories...

THEY ATTENDED Midnight Mass with Louise's mother, and sat in the pew alongside his own family. For some reason, it was a particularly touching ritual tonight. Well, actually, Phillipe did know the reason. Prayer and a faith in God gave people hope that the horror of war would soon end. When the choir sang "Silent Night," many an eye was misted with tears.

Also touching was the tribute to fallen soldiers who had been members of this parish. And then, to Phillipe's surprise, the priest asked everyone to pray for those military men on active duty, and his name was one of those on the list. Frank Rivard, Louise's brother, was also mentioned, although word was that Frank was MIA—missing in action.

They spent Christmas Day at Alma Rivard's cottage, and Phillipe's parents and some of the kids joined them there for a late dinner and an exchange of gifts, most of which were small and inexpensive. He and Louise had pooled their money to buy her mother a pair of slacks, something Louise had been wanting to do for years, and a new winter coat. Her mother scoffed at the idea of wearing pants, but he could tell that she would be trying them on as soon as they left. As for the coat, winters in Louisiana were mild, but occasionally warm outerwear was a necessity.

They gave his parents a set of ducks, of all things. A male and a female. It had been Louise's idea, which turned out to be a big hit. "Duck eggs are the best things fer bakin'," his mother said.

"And roast duck...yum!" his father added, dancing away when his mother tried to swat him. "Do we give them the same feed as the chickens?"

Everyone oohed and aahed over Louise's ring. She couldn't have been prouder if he'd given her a huge rock of a diamond.

Phillipe took lots of pictures with the new camera given to him by his family...his father, mother, and PawPaw...until he ran out of flashbulbs. He promised to take pictures in his travels and send them home, which he probably wouldn't be able to do, but he didn't tell them that. They would drop the film off for developing on Monday, but the photographs wouldn't be ready before he left. Louise would send him copies.

After exclaiming over Louise's ring once again, his mother asked her, "What did you get Phillipe, honey?"

Louise exchanged a glance with Phillipe and blushed. She said, "Oh, just two studio pictures of myself."

"Why didn't you bring them with you?" her mother asked. "Kin I get a copy of one fer framin'?"

"Um, sure," Louise said. But she was probably thinking, *Over my dead body!*

"Yeah, Louise, maybe the studio still has the negatives," Phillipe suggested with a wink.

She gave him a pointed look which translated to,

"You will pay. Later." But all she said in a hushed voice was, "Don't you wink at me."

Louise loved his winks.

And then the days sped by, way too fast. They made love so many times that he had to buy another tin of rubbers from a pharmacy on Canal Street. While he was standing in line waiting for the clerk to replenish the stock on the shelf behind the counter, another guy, an Army sergeant, waiting for the same thing, remarked, "Did you hear about the guy who bought some rubbers from a local pharmacy, and when he showed up for his blind date, he discovered her father was the pharmacist? Ha, ha, ha."

Phillipe just smiled, anxious to get back to Louise. Every waning moment was precious now. Looking around, he decided to buy Louise one of those Whitman Samplers, the fancy kind. She'd told him just last night that the one she stored his letters in was over-flowing. The one he was eyeing now was wooden with a scene painted on top of a bird perched on a branch with lilies or some such flowers. It wasn't cheap, but the look on Louise's face when he gave it to her was well worth an empty pocket and equally empty ration book.

And now it was New Year's Eve, and they were going to the ball being held at the USO near Fort Polk. He was wearing his dress blues, and she was dressed to the nines in a red gown of some material she called chiffon.

After a few hours, Louise looked up at him...they'd

been slow dancing to "Till the End of Time"...and said, "This is fun, Phillipe. Can we leave?"

"My sentiments, exactly."

Back at the cottage by midnight, they were soon in bed. The lovemaking now was desperate, but slow, as the clock ticked down. They probably wouldn't sleep this night.

In between their bouts of lovemaking, they talked.

"When I get back to base, I'm naming you as next of kin," he said.

"No! Don't talk like that."

"It's just a formality, sweetheart. Besides, I haven't got two dimes to rub together. So you'll never get rich off me."

She didn't laugh at his little joke because she knew, as well as he did, that this technicality meant that she would be informed in case something bad happened.

"Will you take the pin-up pictures with you...wherever you're going?" He hadn't told her that he was off to London, but she probably guessed he would be there eventually. All the newspapers mentioned it as a launching point for many U.S. troops. Europe was, after all, where the fighting was taking place.

"Are you kidding? They'll be with me *wherever* I go."

"Oh, I forgot to tell you...my roommates and I are going to pitch our money together to have a phone installed. Will you be able to call me?"

"I should. It might be difficult sometimes, but we'll work something out. That is great news, honey."

"Do you want me to take your car back to your parents' place for storage?"

"Nah. Belle is on her last legs. You drive her till she gives up the ghost. I don't think she's worth any more repairs."

And then, with all the practical things taken care of, he turned to her and said, "You're not the only one who reads books, darlin'. Have I mentioned that we Cajun men have a secret talent, passed down through the generations? Especially if we're lucky enough to have a Cajun girl."

"Oh, really?" she said, always game for something new. "And would this talent involve a certain body part?"

"Um, not at first. Well, not the one you're referring to...what did you call it...*Le Buche.*"

She glanced downward. "The log appears to be sleeping."

"Not for long," he promised. "No, this talent involves a secret erotic place on a woman's body."

"Oh, boy!" she said. Then, "Are you makin' this up, sugar?"

"Not at all." He made a cross mark over his heart. "It's called the Cajun C-spot, and it can only be found with the tongue."

Pillow talk followed later, softly spoken words mixed with sleepy caresses. They didn't mention marriage, but it was understood that a big Cajun wedding would be held on his return. Hopefully, by September which was Louise's favorite month for a wedding.

"Who knew women had favorite months for

weddings? Guys just show up for the event and hope there will be enough booze at the reception," he teased her.

"As long as you show up," she countered with a growl, which he found kind of sexy and which led to other things.

The time for gaiety ended eventually, of course, and he told her, "I will love you forever, Louise. Till the end of time."

"I'll be waiting here for you. Always." She tried her best not to cry, so her voice was wobbly.

And then he left.

But it turned out he was to see Louise again before the big mission. His pawpaw died in April, and Phillipe was given a short liberty to return to the states for the funeral. He was able to spend a few precious hours with Louise at her cottage after the funeral and before his departure at the airport.

This time when he left, he had a bad feeling. He couldn't put a name to it, but if he did, it would be foreboding.

CHAPTER 8

I'll never smile again...

Over the next few months, Louise worked hard, both at the Higgins plant and out at her mother's cottage. She still wrote to Phillipe every day and received numerous letters from him, and occasionally they talked on the phone. She now knew, or guessed, that he was in England because the operator who put through his staticky calls had a decided British accent.

Rumors abounded about what was happening with the war, and the news was not promising. She prayed a lot, and her mother was saying novenas for both Phillipe and Frank, from whom they still had no word.

At the beginning of June, she had a disturbing phone call from Phillipe.

"It will be over soon, sweetheart," he told her.

"Can I start plannin' a wedding?"

"No. Don't want to jinx anything. But soon. I look at your pictures every day and wish I was there with you."

"Me, too. I'm readin' lots more books, if ya get my meaning."

He laughed. "Just so you don't practice on anyone else."

"Never."

"Pray for me...us, will you, Louise?"

Shivers swept over her body at his request. "Of course."

"Love you forever, baby," he ended.

A few days later, in the middle of the night on June 6, one of her roommates awakened her. "What? What is it?"

"My cousin just called. General Eisenhower is about to make an important message on the radio."

Louise grabbed a robe and rushed to the living room where all three of her roommates were huddled around the big console radio. Everyone had a friend or family or loved one involved in this horrid war.

The general said, in what was termed the Order of the Day:

Soldiers, Sailors, and Airmen of the Allied Expeditionary Force!

You are about to embark upon the Great Crusade, toward which we have striven these many months. The eyes of the world are upon you. The hope and prayers of liberty-loving people everywhere march with you. In company with our brave Allies and brothers-in-arms on other Fronts, you will bring about the destruction of the German war machine, the elimination of Nazi tyranny over the oppressed peoples of Europe, and security for ourselves in a free world.

Your task will not be an easy one. Your enemy is well trained, well equipped and battle-hardened. He will fight savagely.

But this is the year 1944! Much has happened since the Nazi triumphs of 1940-41. The United Nations have inflicted upon the Germans great defeats, in open battle, man-to-man. Our air offensive has seriously reduced their strength in the air and their capacity to wage war on the ground. Our Home Fronts have given us an overwhelming superiority in weapons and munitions of war, and placed at our disposal great reserves of trained fighting men. The tide has turned! The free men of the world are marching together to Victory!

I have full confidence in your courage, devotion to duty and skill in battle. We will accept nothing less than full Victory!

Good luck! And let us beseech the blessing of Almighty God upon this great and noble undertaking.

Tears rolled down all their eyes as they pondered the ominousness of the commander's words. Unable to sit still, Louise grabbed a coat and found herself heading toward St. Louis Cathedral on Jackson Square where dozens, maybe hundreds of others, had a like idea.

The next day, the newspapers were full of stories

about what was called D-Day, the most important battle of the war which was taking place at that moment on a beach in Normandy. She went to work where everyone was speculating about the outcome of today's actions, predicting enormous casualties.

Four days later, on a Saturday, Louise was ironing a blouse in the kitchen when the doorbell rang. One of her roommates, Sonia Dullen, the only one home, called out, "I'll get it. I'm expecting a package."

Since silence followed, Louise figured it was the expected delivery. She soon found out that it was a delivery of another sort.

"Louise, can you come here, please?" she heard Sonia say.

She put the iron in its metal rest and made her way toward the living room. Halfway there, she put a hand to her throat and moaned. "Oh, no. No, no, no!" she whimpered.

Standing in the open doorway was one of the "Angels of Death," a telegram delivery boy. The look on his face said it all.

Phillipe was dead.

For the first time in her life, Louise fainted.

∽

The Big Grief begins…

FOR THE NEXT MONTH, Louise felt like one of those

movie zombies. She held herself together until after Phillipe's funeral service, but her body was numb. She became a wooden, emotionless creature who performed everyday duties: bathing, eating, working, but just barely.

Her mother made the trek into New Orleans one Saturday in late July, hitching a ride with a neighbor who had a doctor's appointment. She found Louise in her bedroom, where she often stayed when not at work, lying in a fetal position. She was tired, always so tired. Her roommates had gone to some parade being held in the French Quarter for returning soldiers. They'd given up on urging her to come out with them.

"Girl, this has got to stop. Get yerself up off that bed and straighten out."

"I doan want to, Mama. I just want to sleep."

"I got word about Frank," her mother announced. "He died in some prison camp."

She realized that her mother's red-rimmed eyes weren't just for Phillipe then. Her only son was gone. "Oh, Mama!" Louise forced herself to sit up. "I'm so sorry." She'd never been close to Frank, who was so much older, but she felt for her mother's pain. Would the death and destruction from that horrid war never end?

"I suspected he was gone, when we dint hear from him fer so long, even when the POWs were released right after the war. Still..." Her mother swiped at her eyes with a handkerchief and sat down on the bed next to her. Putting an arm around Louise's shoulders, she tugged her close and said, "We're all we got now, of our family. Jist you and me."

"Will there be a service?"

Her mother nodded. "Next week. You'll be there, won't you?"

"I will," Louise promised, although how she would garner the energy, or be able to sit through another funeral Mass with all its reminders of Phillipe, she had no idea.

"Lots of people have lost loved ones in the war, honey. They grieve, but they go on. Thass what we have ta do, both of us."

"My grief is too big. It surrounds me, it's inside me, it consumes me."

"Oh, chile, why doan ya come stay with me fer awhile? The bayou is the best place fer healin'."

Louise shook her head. "We need the money from my job."

"Trust in God, thass what I allus say."

"Where was He when Phillipe was dying on that beach? Or Frank was dying in some prison camp?"

"Hush, child! You know better than that."

She wasn't going to argue religion with her mother. Not now. But back to that other question. "I can't quit my job, Mama. Every penny counts, you know that."

"We can get by on less. We're Cajuns, honey. Survivors."

"No, Mama. Maybe sometime later, but for now I have to hold onto this job." In truth, she didn't know what she would do without it. Just sleep all day? Or stumble through the streets where she'd walked with Phillipe? Pass the hotel where they'd first made love? No, too many memories!

Louise did straighten out after that, to some extent, except she took what she now thought of as her Big Grief in a new direction. It started one night when her roommates talked her into going out with them to a popular club. Staring at herself in the mirror of the bathroom medicine cabinet, she used a pair of shears to clip off all the wavy tresses of her dark hair. Phillipe had loved her hair long. Then, donning the tightest dress she owned and the highest pumps, she vowed to forget her past, if only for one night.

After that, she became a loose woman, drinking until her brain shut down. Sleeping with men, lots of men, nameless men. On the outside, she looked like a wilder, more outrageous version of her old self. Fun-loving. Reckless. Inside, she was sick.

She hated herself and what she was doing, but she couldn't stop. Until one morning she awakened in bed with a snoring man she didn't know. They were both naked, lying on a bare mattress with stains she didn't dare examine too closely. With a pounding headache and so nauseated she had to clap a hand over her mouth, she barely made it to a filthy bathroom and vomited the contents of her stomach. She'd been doing that a lot lately, and losing weight at an alarming rate. Even her roommates had noticed and urged her to see a doctor.

I don't need a doctor to tell me I'm dying, bit by bit. Of heartbreak. She wasn't suicidal, but life had no meaning for her anymore.

Looking down at the toilet, which hadn't seen a brush since the Civil War, she recognized this as a new low for her. Rinsing out her mouth, not bothering to comb her unruly hair, which was a cap of dark curls these days, she donned the wrinkled clothes from the previous night that lay about the floor, where she noticed a cockroach scurrying across the linoleum. *Welcome to my world, bug,* she thought. An Army uniform lay over a straight-back chair, and that felt like a betrayal of sorts to Phillipe...that she would give herself to another soldier. *Can I feel any lower?* The man, whoever he was, was still snoring when she left.

Still feeling the effects of last night's alcohol—*Did I really down eight Sazerac cocktails on a challenge from someone at Buster's Beer Garden?*—she stumbled her way outside, recognizing the street, one of the seedier ones in the Quarter. With no apparent destination in mind, she found herself in Jackson Square, facing St. Louis Cathedral. She sank down onto a stone bench. She couldn't face entering the church at this point, even if she had the inclination, which she didn't. God did not fit into the parameters of her hopeless life anymore.

"No one is hopeless," a male voice said.

Huh? Was I talking out loud? She turned and saw that a man was sitting beside her. When had that happened, or had he been here first?

She blinked her bleary eyes, which were irritated by the bright sunlight. It must be almost noon. She couldn't remember what day it was, but that would come to her, in time. No, she knew. It was Saturday. No work today. Thank God!

"And so thou should thank God. For many things," the man remarked.

Now this was getting ridiculous. She knew she hadn't spoken aloud that time. Giving him a closer look, she almost laughed. The guy wore a long white robe, tied at the waist with a rope belt. And he had a long wooden walking stick, longer than a cane. A staff, that's what it was. How she knew that, she wasn't sure, and her brain was too sodden with booze to care.

"Are you a priest?" Didn't some priests wear robes like this under their vestments? Cassocks, they were called. He must have come from the cathedral. "Or are you in a choir or something?"

He shook his head. "Neither. I am an apostle."

And I'm Betty Grable. "What's your name?"

"'Tis Jude. Jude Thaddeus."

Oh, this is just great, on this day of new lows, I have to meet up with a wacko. And what was with the "thou" and "'tis" language? "St. Jude?"

He nodded.

She laughed.

He didn't even crack a smile. "Some say I am the patron saint of hopeless cases."

"Well, you certainly came ta the right place. That's me. Miss Hopeless."

"Tsk-tsk-tsk! When will people understand that nothing happens but what God wills?"

"Bullshit!" she swore, uncaring if he was a saint or a

119

crazy escapee from an asylum. "Are you sayin' that God willed Phillipe ta die?"

He shrugged.

"I'm not buyin' it."

"Mayhap someday thou wilt understand. But verily I say unto you, the life God wants for you is not down the path thou hast chosen. He has a plan for you, child." He gave her a head-to-toe scrutiny that was not complimentary.

She must look a mess, and she probably smelled. "I doubt that."

"As did Thomas."

"Huh?"

"Phillipe sent me."

Louise gasped. "How do you know...what do you mean?"

"Phillipe is in a good place, but he worries about you."

Oh, this was cruel. A cruel joke.

"Not a joke," the man said, placing a hand over hers.

Once again, she knew that she hadn't spoken aloud. How had he read her mind? And what was it with that odd warmth emanating from his hand to hers? She edged away from him on the bench, suddenly frightened.

"Fear not, Louise. God has blessed you." He was gazing at her belly.

Was he trying to say...? Was it possible...? "Oh, no! None of that immaculate conception stuff!"

"Hardly applicable in your case," the man...Jude... said with a note of wry humor.

"Are you saying I'm pregnant? I mean, Phillipe always used..." She didn't finish her sentence but he knew what she meant.

"Only God is infallible. Didst not learn such in catechism class?"

If she *was* pregnant, what if the child wasn't Phillipe's? Louise bowed her head. "I feel so hopeless."

He squeezed her hand and said, "That is why I am here. You are never to feel hopeless again."

"But..." She blinked away the tears that misted her eyes, then did a double take. There was no one there. She'd been talking to herself.

However, she noticed a long stick propped against the bench.

On Monday morning, she sat in a doctor's office, listening to her diagnosis. "You are five months pregnant, Louise," Dr. Fenton said.

"How is it possible that I'm five months pregnant, and didn't know? I've lost weight, not gained."

"It happens," the doctor said with a shrug. "A stealth or cryptic pregnancy, it's called. One of the causes is stress, and you've certainly had that with the loss of your fiancé." Louise had told him about Phillipe in the initial interview.

Louise put a hand to her flat stomach. "Does that mean something's wrong?"

"Not at all. You'll get a bump eventually, probably soon."

Five months, Louise pondered. The baby was Phillipe's then. She exhaled on a sigh of relief.

"You've got to put on some pounds now, for the baby, if not for your own health. Eat more, even if you're not hungry. And eat healthy."

Louise nodded. *And no more alcohol or wild living,* she told herself.

"Will you keep the baby? I can give you a list of agencies that could help with adoptions, if you're interested."

"No! This is Phillipe's child. I will cherish him... her...it." A bubble of laughter erupted in her. She couldn't remember the last time she'd smiled, let alone laughed. *A baby! I'm going to have Phillipe's baby.*

"It will be difficult raising an illegitimate child," the doctor cautioned. "No, don't be offended. I'm just warning you that, even in these times, an unwed mother is a scandal."

"I don't care! Can't you see? I'm going to have Phillipe's baby. That's all I care about."

Leaving the doctor's office, she felt as if she'd been given a reason for living. Maybe that man in Jackson Square had been right. Maybe Phillipe *was* worried about her, wherever he was, and he'd sent her this miracle. Oh, she hoped so! It shamed her to think that Phillipe might know what she'd been doing since his death, but she resolved to do better now. She had a reason to change, a reason for living.

Later that day, she drove Phillipe's old clunker to her mother's house on Bayou Black. Apparently, her mother saw something on her face as she emerged from the car because she put her hand to her heart and said, "What? What is it?"

"I'm going to have Phillipe's baby, Mama."

Instead of being shocked or condemning her for promiscuity, her mother opened her arms to Louise and hugged her tightly. They wept on each other's shoulders, but they were tears of bittersweet happiness.

That didn't mean her mother had no concerns. She did, and later she passed them on to Louise. Sitting down to a glass of sweet tea and a slice of Figgy Buttermilk Cake, freshly made, her mother cautioned, "The baby will be illegitimate, and ya know what the bayou is like. Now, doan be getting' yer back up, we gotta be talkin' practical here."

"Practical be damned!"

"That kinda language won't accomplish nothin'."

"What do ya suggest I do, Mama? Go out and find a man ta marry me just ta give the baby a name?"

"No, but—"

"I'm not givin' my baby...Phillipe's baby...up fer adoption."

"I never expected ya would."

"Well, then?"

"We need a plan."

"Ya mean, I go away like some girls did in high school, and then come back six ta nine months later with a baby, claimin' I got married? No one believes those stories."

"No, we gotta do better than that." Her mother seemed to be thinking. "How 'bout in a month or two, when ya begin ta show, ya quit yer job, citin' yer Big Grief...thass what ya call it, isn't it? While they think yer

123

takin' a break, ya kin go ta one of those homes fer unwed mothers. There's one in Biloxi run by the Sisters of Divine Light, I think."

Louise cringed at the idea of sitting around with a bunch of other pregnant women, crying over their sad situations. On the other hand, it would give her a sanctuary, a place to hide out for a while.

"While yer gone, I could put the word out that ya went ta Mexico where Frank's widow, Patti Rivard, is about ta have a baby."

"Patti's pregnant?"

"Louise! Pay attention. No, Patti's not pregnant, far as I know. Anyways, when ya return with yer baby, we would say it was Frank's and Patti's, and that yer gonna raise it...that Patti has a new life with a new man who doesn't want any reminders of her husband."

"Hmmm," Louise said. "That might work. Since Patti ran off with that AWOL soldier even before Frank was captured, she probably wouldn't want to be saddled with Frank's baby, if she really was pregnant."

"Supposedly, she's livin' in Mexico now. She has no family in these parts. So, chances are no one would ever know," her mother went on.

"That would mean that the baby would consider you its grandmother, but I would only ever be its aunt."

Her mother shrugged. "A small price ta pay, dontcha think? And ya kin allus tell the chile the truth later on."

Louise shook her head. "No, if we go ahead with this crazy plan, I'll start as I mean ta go on."

Thus it was that Adèle Rivard was born on January

1, 1946. And a new chapter began in the life of Louise Rivard.

When Adèle was one year old and beginning to talk, she was unable to manage Aunt Louise, or Tante Louise. Instead, she babbled the words, "Tante Lulu." And the name stuck.

One day, Louise remarked when watching her daughter romp in the backyard by the bayou, "Y'know, Mama, no matter what the future holds, I'll always have a bit of Phillipe that lives on. Till we meet again."

"Thank God!" her mother replied

Ahem! a voice in Louise's head said. *Art thou forgetting someone? Am I a potted tupelo tree here?*

With a smile, Louise recalled the man in Jackson Square. "And thank St. Jude."

CHAPTER 9

Present day.
Back to the future...

I'm not dead.

>   *Well, that's a relief.*

It *was a dream.*

Darn it!

But what a dream! It was wonderful seeing Phillipe again. Being with him. And, holy crawfish, I was a hottie back then! I forgot that I looked that good.

Louise drifted in a dream state, slowly coming awake to awareness of her surroundings, even though her eyes were still closed. She had fainted, of all things, right out in public, in the middle of that big war event.

I knew it was a mistake. I shoulda stayed home and made fig preserves.

But, no, then I wouldn't have met up with Phillipe again.

Oh, Lordy, I hope I wasn't moanin' when we were havin' dream sex.

She scrooched her hiney around a little and realized that she was lying on some kind of cot. Probably in that medical tent they'd passed a bit ago.

Then voices intruded on her dream...thoughts... whatever. They appeared be hovering over her. She recognized Luc, Réne, and Remy, her three nephews.

No, not nephews. Grandsons. All these years, and I never revealed my secret. Should I tell them now? Would it matter if they know? Would it make them think less of me?

No, I've lived too long being their loving aunt. Maybe when I go to my Final Reward, I'll leave a note informing them of their actual bloodlines. One of those Last Will and Testament Big Reveals that would shock everyone.

Then again, maybe not.

Suddenly, Phillipe was standing next to her. Apparently, the dream wasn't over yet. He took her hand and gazed down at the three men. "We did good, didn't we, darlin'?"

She turned to look at him. He was so handsome in his Navy dress uniform, the one he'd been buried in, and he was young, too, same age as when he'd died. But then, glancing down at the smooth skin of her hand, minus the "Flowers of Death," or liver spots, that adorned her flesh now, she realized that she was young, too.

She must be dead, after all.

"Oh, Phillipe, are we going to finally be together again?"

"Not yet."

Disappointment flooded her. "But I've missed you so much!"

"And I've missed you even more. Someday, we'll be together, my love. But now is not your time."

"Why?"

"You have work to do yet."

"I do? The figs kin rot fer all I care."

"Not that," he said with a smile. "Your family...*our* family...needs you."

"Are there going to be more babies?"

"That's not for me to say."

"Wait. Don't go away. There's so much—"

"Shhh. Till we meet again, darlin'."

He faded away, and voices speaking above and around her became louder. Intrusive. Demanding.

"I think she's just taking a nap."

"In the middle of a thousand people at this blasted fair?"

"Why not? It would be just like her. She loves to be the center of attention."

"Is she dead?" someone asked.

"No, she's breathin'."

"But why isn't she wakin' up?"

"I know what will get the old bird's attention." It was René speaking, she could tell. And she was going to give him "old bird" with a whack of her St. Jude fan when she got up. "Hey, Tante Lulu," René said in an overloud voice, "I think I see Richard Simmons over there. He's teachin' Radio Josette how ta do jumpin' jacks."

"Yer a bunch of idjits," she said, sitting up and brushing off Remy's hand when he tried to help her stand. As her family, all eighteen of them, clustered around her, she tried to figure who might be in trouble or in need of her matchmaking services.

There was Mary Lou, a Cajun cowgirl if there ever was one, spending way too much time on her daddy's ranch with horses, instead of men. Or Luc's three daughters. Andy LeDeux, the New Orleans Saints player, nicknamed "Candy Andy" because he was such great... well, eye candy, didn't need any help from her in attracting women; in fact, she might need to weed out ninety-nine per cent of his "harem" if he didn't get down to business soon.

But wait. She knew exactly who needed her most. Etienne-Call-Me-Steve. She smiled, and heard someone say, "Uh-oh! Tante Lulu has her wicked smile on. She's plannin' something. Guar-an-teed!"

She glanced over at Etienne, who was staring at her with concern. He was a good boy, despite his wild ways, bless his heart. Even so, he was too young to be one of her prospects anytime soon. It was hopeless to think she could hold on till he was of an age.

But then she heard a voice in her head say, *Hopeless? Did someone say hopeless? Bite thy tongue, lady.*

And so the Tante Lulu adventures would go on.

THE END
(for now)

FIGGY BUTTERMILK CAKE

Ingredients for cake:

- 2 cups flour
- ¾ cup oil (preferably canola)
- 1-2 cups chopped figs (or fig preserves)
- 1 ½ cups granulated sugar
- ½ cup brown sugar
- 3 eggs, beaten
- 1 cup buttermilk
- 1 tsp vanilla
- 1 tsp baking soda
- 1 tsp cinnamon
- 1 tsp nutmeg
- 1 tsp cloves
- 1 tsp salt
- 1 cup chopped pecans or walnuts (optional)

(Ingredients continue on next page)

Ingredients for the glaze:

- ¼ cup buttermilk
- ¼ cup butter, softened
- ½ cup granulated sugar
- 1 ½ tsp corn starch
- ¼ tsp baking soda
- 1 tsp vanilla
- 2 tsp syrup, optional (corn or molasses)

Directions for cake:

Mix together the beaten eggs, oil, sugars, and vanilla. Gradually add the flour, baking soda, spices. Then the buttermilk. Fold in the figs and nuts. Spread into a greased and floured cake pan (9 x 13) or a Bundt cake pan. Bake at 350 degrees for 50-60 minutes, until a toothpick comes out clean. Glaze the cake while it is warm, and possibly again when it cools, if so desired.

Directions for buttermilk glaze:

Heat together in a sauce pan the sugar, baking soda, corn starch, butter, and buttermilk (and syrup, optional) until it comes to a low boil, stirring constantly. Remove from heat. It should be smooth and fluffy. Spread onto the top (and sides, if a Bundt) of the warm cake. If desired, spread again when cool. Can be served with ice cream, whipped cream, or alone.

READER LETTER

Dear Readers:

I hope you liked Tante Lulu's story. It was a long time coming.

It can be read as a stand-alone book. Or, in chronological order in terms of the Cajun series, it would be between CAJUN CRAZY and CAJUN PERSUASION (coming in the summer of 2018).

If you haven't tried my Cajun books before (Shame on you! <g>), you should start with THE LOVE POTION. Lots of people don't realize that it was the first book, and the first appearance of Tante Lulu, because it was originally published by a now-defunct company. It has since been reissued, of course.

That book was followed by TALL, DARK, AND CAJUN; THE CAJUN COWBOY; THE RED-HOT CAJUN; PINK JINX; PEARL JINX; WILD JINX; SO

INTO YOU (BAYOU ANGEL); SNOW ON THE BAYOU; THE CAJUN DOCTOR; CAJUN CRAZY; and CAJUN PERSUASION. Whew! I never intended there to be so many books when I first started writing about the beloved bayou country.

It should be noted that I am not from the South, although I fell in love with Louisiana while accompanying my husband on several business trips there. I feel such an empathy for that region that I wondered if some of my ancestors might have been Southerners, a sort of genetic memory. Alas, the answer is no. However, I should point out that my grandmother, whose maiden name was Butler, always said she was related to Rhett Butler. I know, I know, dear old Rhett was a fictional character. Still...

It should also be noted that my oldest son is named Beau, a Southern name to be sure. My husband insisted on that name, for reasons still unknown.

Let me know what you think of Tante Lulu's story by contacting me at my website, SandraHill.net, or on my Facebook page at Sandra Hill Author. As always, I wish you smiles in your reading, and Tante Lulu wishes you *joie de vivre.*

Sandra Hill

ABOUT THE AUTHOR

Sandra Hill is the best-selling author of almost fifty novels and the recipient of numerous awards. She has appeared on many bestseller lists, including the *New York Times* and *USA Today*.

Readers love the trademark humor in her books, whether the heroes are Vikings, Cajuns, Navy SEALs, treasure hunters, or vangels (Viking vampire angels), and they tell her so often, sometimes with letters that are laugh-out-loud funny. In addition, her fans feel as if they know the characters in her books on a personal basis, especially the outrageous Tante Lulu.

At home in central Pennsylvania with her husband, four sons, a dog the size of a horse, six dogs belonging to her sons, and three grandchildren, Sandra is always busy. When she is not at their home, so close to the Penn State football stadium that she can hear the Blue Band practicing every night, she can be found relaxing at their Spruce Creek cottage.

Sandra is always on the lookout for new sources of humor. So be careful if you run into Sandra. What you say or do may end up in a book. If you want to take the chance, you can contact her at SandraHill.net. She loves to hear from her fans.

ALSO BY SANDRA HILL

Sandra Hill's Cajun Novels (In Order):

The Love Potion

Tall, Dark, and Cajun

The Cajun Cowboy

The Red-Hot Cajun

Pink Jinx

Pearl Jinx

Wild Jinx

So Into You (Bayou Angel)

Snow on the Bayou

The Cajun Doctor

Cajun Crazy

Cajun Persuasion

Novellas

"Jinx Christmas" in A Dixie Christmas Anthology

"Saving Savannah" in Heart Craving Anthology

"When Lulu was Hot"

CPSIA information can be obtained
at www.ICGtesting.com
Printed in the USA
BVHW032201041220
594951BV00012B/198

9 781941 528556